T0110275

THE LONG WAIT

THE LONG WAIT

Dr. Anwarul Haque

PARTRIDGE
A Penguin Random House Company

Copyright © 2014 by Dr. Anwarul Haque.

ISBN: Softcover   978-1-4828-1767-6
               Ebook   978-1-4828-1768-3

All rights reserved. No part of this book may be used or reproduced by any means, graphic, electronic, or mechanical, including photocopying, recording, taping or by any information storage retrieval system without the written permission of the publisher except in the case of brief quotations embodied in critical articles and reviews.

Because of the dynamic nature of the Internet, any web addresses or links contained in this book may have changed since publication and may no longer be valid. The views expressed in this work are solely those of the author and do not necessarily reflect the views of the publisher, and the publisher hereby disclaims any responsibility for them.

To order additional copies of this book, contact
Partridge India
000 800 10062 62
www.partridgepublishing.com/india
orders.india@partridgepublishing.com

This book is dedicated to my beloved wife
Shabana Naz

Acknowledgement

In the preparation of *The Long Wait,* the entire team of Dynamic Training Services Pvt. Ltd. motivated me to accomplish the book including its directors, Mr. Jonathan C. Shifley and Mrs. Heather Shifley, and the teachers of Dynamic, including Mr. Randall Long and Mrs. Heidi Long. I am indebted to Ms. Michelle Lyons for her help and support. Being the first reader of the book, she not only encouraged me to publish the novel, but also edited it and made it publishable. I must say that without her help this book could not have been possible.

I would like to thank my father, Syed Rezaul Haque, my children, Azhanul Haque, Sarah Khairi, and Ahsanul Haque; my wife, Shabana Naz, and the teachers at the Department of Urdu Jamia Millia Islamia, including Prof. Khalid Mahmood, Prof. Shehpar Rasool, Dr. Khalid Javed, Dr. Ahmad Mahfooz, Dr. Kausar Mazhari, Dr. Suhail A. Farooqi, Dr. Nadim Ahmad, Dr. Imran

A. Andaleeb, Dr. Sarwarul Hoda, and Dr. Khalid Mubashshir. My special thanks to my M.phil. and Ph. D. Supervisor, Prof. Wahajuddin Alvi, for his blessings and guidance. My friends with the Tagore Research and Translation Scheme, Dr. Mashkoor Moini, Dr. Fareha Bano, Mr. Mohsin Ali Khan, and Dr. H. M. Imran and the coordinator of the TRTS project Prof. Shahzad Anjum are worthy of being saluted because of their love and support towards me.

This book is a work of fiction. Names, characters, places and incidents either are products of the author's imagination or are used fictitiously. Any resemblance to actual events or locales or persons, living or dead, is entirely coincidental.

Dr. Anwarul Haque
New Delhi
December 25, 2013

Chapter One

She lost her balance while trying to control her slipper with her weak foot. Her slipper came off and went into the canal, where she could see it floating. She tried to get it out without any help from her friends—she was very independent. She was only thirteen, had one atrophied leg, and she could hardly move her neck because of a strange viral disease called Poliomyelitis.

She never liked it when other people helped her, only when she had no option left. That was a new pink slipper, which her father bought her that morning. He could not find any cheaper than this one, but still she liked it a lot and was very happy.

She was trying hard to reach down into the canal to get the slipper out, but she failed. The canal was behind her village, almost a half mile away. Usually four or five girls went to play there. Every day in the evening they used to go to play *kit-kit* on the dam.

1

When a girl saw her slipping into the canal, she along with four other girls began shouting and running towards her. One girl hauled her up to the dam. Another took a stick that was lying there and with the help of that she fished out the pink slipper. Her face glowed with joy as she saw the slipper in one of her friend's hands.

"You were going to lose your life just for this cheap slipper, Rani," a friend, who was wearing nice leather slippers, commented. Rani noticed and replied, "My younger brother has much better slippers than yours."

"I am not criticizing your slipper ok," her friend stressed on K and advised. "I mean to say that the slipper is not more valuable than your life. You might have drowned. Can't you think?" She spoke with a bit of anger.

Rani seemed a little sorry for her because she knew that her friends cared for her. They became busy in playing again. A boy of the same age as her came running up to the girls and stopped. He held his breath and stood up. He had no slippers on his feet. Roaming in the village without slippers was very common. He was wearing a torn shirt, which was also common for those kids.

"Hello! What are you doing here? Go home! Move! Move! Let us play." The girls felt a little uncomfortable playing in the presence of that boy.

"Rani, you are playing here with your friends while some policemen came to your home this evening and arrested your father and took him to jail," the boy informed them.

Rani and her friends were shocked to hear this and ran towards the village. When they reached the village, they saw many people gathered at her house, talking to one another. Her mother, along with her brothers, was screaming and shouting (and of course using some swear words) at her uncle, who was sitting next to the door, widening his chest, behaving like a winner busy in talking with four or five people around him. Rani was too young to understand everything.

The people who had gathered inside the house of Rani's father were trying to make strategies to get him out of jail. Her father was not a criminal. There was some conspiracy against him. Only two hours had passed when a police officer riding a motorcycle came by and asked for Rani's mother.

"Where is Hamid's wife? I want to talk to her right now!" The police officer roared while he brushed his big mustache with his right hand. He parked his motorcycle and stood under a *neem* tree. As soon as he came, all of the villagers stood around him. A little boy ran up with a chair for him and an old man cleaned the chair with his towel. The police officer sat there like a king. Hamid's wife came. Her face was partially covered with a sari and she was crying.

"Sir, please save my husband. He is innocent and he was framed. We would be very thankful to you. We have small kids . . ." That was all she could say in a broken voice and then she began screaming. Two more women held her while she was beating her chest.

"Stop all this drama!" the police officer said and looked around at the people. "Red shirt . . . you, yes, I am talking to you." He rolled his eyes pretending like he was very angry. People started looking at each other and whispering together. The man wearing the red shirt came forward. He was frightened.

"What is it, sir?" He was very scared.

"Come here," the police officer, scolded him.

When he came near, the police officer stood up and slapped him. "Why did you take so long to come?" he asked angrily. Then, stressing each word, he commanded, "Go and get a glass of water for me."

"Yes sir," the man said and ran away. After this incident, the people became very quiet. They even stopped whispering.

The police officer again sat on the chair like the Mughal emperor Akbar, who used to sit after sentencing capital punishment or after any other cruel decision.

"See, a very severe case has been lodged against your husband. Understand? He can be punished for more than five years, maybe even ten years. Even I don't know as it all depends on the court. Think about how you would live without him," the police officer advised her.

"The case is in my hands right now but once it is out of my control, I will not be able to do anything. The sub-inspector is very strict but I will try to convince him for you. However, why should I do all this for you?" The police officer left the puzzle unsolved.

She became very inquisitive. "Sir, please suggest what I should do," she said with curiosity.

"If you insist then I will try," the police officer said, becoming a little more polite. "But you might have to pay for it. Official work is very expensive nowadays. Minimum, you need to pay five thousand bucks if you want your husband back in the next five days."

"Five days! Is there not any other way to get him back early?"

"Hmm, let me see. I can't make a commitment . . ."

The police officer spoke in her ear. "If you will not disclose to anyone about the money you are paying me, then he will be freed by tonight." he whispered.

"But I don't have any money, sir."

"No problem then. I cannot do anything. Tomorrow morning the van will take him to the district jail, and then you will need to go to court every day to fight for justice. No one knows how long he will stay in jail. Poor Hamid!" the police officer showed Hamid's future to her. She told the police officer to wait there for some time and went inside the house where Chand Mia was waiting for her.

"What happened?" Chand Mia asked curiously.

"He is asking for money."

"What did you say?"

"Nothing yet."

"Why? You should have said yes."

"But I have no cash available at home."

"No worries. If you have jewelry available then I can arrange a mortgage for you at a low interest rate. Remember, at this time, nothing is more important than your husband." Chand Mia offered to help her. Then, she went inside, came back with a small packet of jewelry, and handed it over to the police officer. And thanked him in a broken voice.

A clever smile appeared on his face. Chand Mia went away after that.

Next door, the person was very happy and in Hamid's house, the situation was very tense. The person next door was Hamid's elder brother Rashid.

That night around eight o'clock, the police officer called Hamid and ordered him to go because the paper work was done and someone had arranged his bail. Hamid was curious to know who the person was that had helped him but the police told him that it was his wife. When he was coming out after signing the papers, he saw that Chand Mia was talking to the policemen and in a jolly mood. They all held a glass in their hands and a bottle of vodka was there on the table. Everybody seemed drunk to him.

At home, Rani's mother was very worried because neither had her husband returned nor had Chand Mia returned. It was very quiet all over. The chair was still lying under the giant neem tree. The tree looked wicked because of the pitch-dark night. Many bird-nests were there in the tree so it looked haunted. At the end of the village, there was a very old mosque. Nobody knew exactly when it had been built. Next to the mosque, there was a large graveyard, the final destination of the villagers.

There was no electricity in this village. However, all the villages around it were fortunate to have electricity because of the Indian government reservation rules. This village did not fall in the reserved category. In every house, kerosene lanterns were hanging to fight off the darkness. The people who could not even afford them usually took a small bottle, made a little hole in the lid, made a little rope with cloth, inserted one end into the hole and left the other end in the bottle. After that, they filled the bottle half way with kerosene oil. This is how they prepared their handmade lamps. They called it a *chiragh* (a Persian word) and they hung it on their terraces.

Hamid was on his way home. He had many things to worry about. Why did the police arrest him when it was not his fault? What would Rani think about all this? Right now, how worried would his wife be? How proud would his brother Rashid be feeling about this incident? What should his next step be now? He was thinking about so many questions. He crossed half of the way playing with all these puzzles. He stepped into a little drain. "Oops, bull shit! All this happens only to me," he said as he pulled his leg out and tried to clean his muddy trousers. He saw a hand pump near the road. He cleaned up and again started down the road then he was passing through a graveyard. He was always afraid whenever he saw the graveyard. It was not because he was afraid of death but because of the many supernatural stories that he had heard about graveyards. There was a very famous shrine in this graveyard named "*Mazar-e-Baba Baqar Shaheed.*" He stopped for a minute, turned his face towards the shrine, closed his eyes and pronounced something for a minute then moved towards the way home.

The people of the entire village were sleeping except his wife who was waiting for him. The greatest benefit of having no electricity was that people went to sleep early. Finally, he reached home at about ten o'clock at night. His wife brought dinner for him. He took some water and splashed it on his face. The *chiragh* blinking at his door had no fuel. On Rashid's door the lantern was lit. Street dogs started barking on the road whenever they saw any bikes or cyclist passing through.

"What did you think about all that?" Hamid's wife asked curiously.

"About what?" Hamid questioned.

"About dinner," she replied with naughtiness.

He looked at her with question marks in his eyes. She was smiling.

Both laughed.

"About the case?"

"No."

"Then?"

"About money."

"Which money?"

"The money I paid to get you out of jail."

"How much was it?"

"Five thousand."

"Five thousand? Where did you get that much money from?"

"From Chand Mia."

"Chand Mia!"

"I can't believe that son of a bi**h . . . gave you that much money for me!"

"You are right. Actually, I gave my jewelry to him."

"What? Did you sell the jewelry to him?"

"No. I gave it to him at the rate of five percent interest."

"Umm . . . ok, mortgage. Why did you do that? I know it was valuable."

"Nothing is more valuable than you, though." She came closer to him and kissed him.

"Ok. Now go to sleep quickly because you need to wake up early tomorrow morning. You need to talk to Rani's teacher. She might ask for the tuition fees," she reminded him.

"How much would that be?" he asked.

"Approx 10 bucks."

"Ok. Pay her tomorrow and tell her not to come from tomorrow onwards."

"But why?"

"Ok. Let's sleep it's too late to discuss this now" he said then he pulled the blanket up to avoid further discussion. His wife understood this and planned to discuss it later.

Rani had not learnt how to read and write yet except to read the Quran and she could hardly read and write Urdu.

Hamid's father was a highly educated and respected person in their village and the villages nearby. At the time he died, Hamid was a teenager so he could not get more education. Since then, his elder brother Rashid had taken care of his two brothers Hamid and Zahid. Because he took care of them in their childhood, he therefore wanted his expenses to be paid back. Rashid had five sons and he was proud of having them.

Hamid had four kids. The first one was Rani, the second one was Abid, the third one was Jawed and the fourth one was a girl named Leila. With time, everything passed but the hours Hamid had spent in jail he could not forget. Hamid had enough land to grow food for his family. When the land properties were divided among the three brothers, the eldest brother, Rashid, tried to acquire more properties than he should get. Eventually, the other brothers began opposing his greed. This was when the legal fight started. Very soon, it became a matter of pride and all three tried to defame each other from day to day. The legal fight became more important than family matters like children's education, career growth, etc. This was not unusual according to the tradition of the fathers and forefathers of most of the middle class families.

For a mother, nothing is more important than her children's careers so Hamid's wife was always concerned about her kids.

The next morning when Hamid woke up, his wife again started the same story.

"Why are you stopping the kids' education? Is the fighting in the court more important to you than the children's education?" she asked with a little anger and in forceful way.

"Why do you want her to study? She is a girl. She is not going to earn money for you in your old age. Moreover, she is handicapped. We need to worry about her marriage. Very soon, she is going to turn fourteen. Do you think it will be easy to find a perfect match for her?

No. It will be very difficult. Who will marry this lame girl? We have male kids Abid and Jawed. We will give them enough education and that will be a good investment for our future. This is my final decision and I will not argue with you about this anymore. Ok?" Hamid almost scolded her.

Hamid's wife almost cried because she could not do anything. This was the only way for a good ideal wife to blindly follow whatever her husband said. She had many dreams for her daughter who was falling down and she was unable to do anything. That morning, Rani woke up because her parents argued loudly and she heard everything her parents were discussing. She was not so young that she did not understand the discussion. She was also angry but could not share her feelings with her parents.

She wanted to share all this with her friends as soon as possible. However, she could not meet her friends so early in the morning because all of them were studying.

"Should I talk to my mother about it? No. She is already upset so I should not make her more worried," she thought.

"What should I do? It's better to pretend as if I didn't hear anything. After all, there was nothing wrong in what my father said. I am a lame girl and I can't help my parents. I have no right to make them more worried. There is no benefit of studying for a girl because I am going to get married and then my job will be handling all of the kitchen related matters. Soon my parents are going to have a hard time finding a groom for me," she thought. She lay on the bed with her eyes closed. Her cheeks were wet with tears. She felt the warmth of her mother's finger on her head. Her mother brushed her hair softly.

Rani wiped her face, got up and hugged her mother. Her mother patted her back.

Hamid was still busy planning to deal with his big bro Rashid. He had no time for kids. Though he pretended to be worried about his son's education, he had no time to think about it. He had arranged a meeting with his lawyer and had to discuss the partition suit of his land property.

Hamid had been sent to jail because of the false allegation filed by Rashid. Now Hamid was planning to pay his brother back by hook, or by crook. This was his only dream for now. He could not forget the insult of being sent to jail.

Their village was not very big. There were almost two hundred houses in the village. There was a giant building in the middle of the village named "Haji House" built by Haji Naim, the father of three brothers Hamid, Zahid and Rashid. Hamid's house was the middle one. The left side was owned by Zahid and Rashid's house was the one of the right side. Rashid's house was a little bigger than Hamid's and Zahid's because he had acquired more land for himself dishonestly. The rest of the entire village was spread over almost the equal amount of land as these three houses. When Haji Naim was alive, no one had the courage to pass through this house without saluting him. It was not done out of fear but out of respect. Haji Naim always helped all of the villagers whenever they need it.

He had built two wells through which all of the villagers used to quench their thirst and still in this twenty first century, they have only these wells for their water needs. That respect had now became a story of the past. The villagers used to respect these three brothers as well but since they started fighting like anything, they had lost that dignity. The village was populated on both sides of the road, one after another, cheek-by-jowl. Behind the village, as far as one could see, there was nothing except fields. However, the dam of the canal could be seen at the end on the west side.

The first concern of Hamid and his family was to take revenge on Rashid and the second concern was Rani's wedding. At least for Hamid, these two concerns were greater than America's mission to arrest Osama bin Laden. Rani was happy in all situations. She always had the questions in her mind of who would take care of every one at home and how would all the work be done without her. After she got married, Mom would be alone and she would have to do everything on her own. Rani's mother always worried about Hamid, his craziness about his revenge, and the education of her children. One day, she lashed out to him about Abid's education but he was not ready to listen to her. As usual, he kept saying that he could not afford it right now but this time his wife won the discussion and convinced him to send Abid to the Madrasa.

Chapter Two

Meanwhile, Hamid's father-in-law came by. He was a teacher in a government school and had many connections with government officials. He proposed to Hamid that if they would donate a piece of land to the village for a primary school then they would get a fabulous benefit.

"A piece of land will give your village a primary school," his father-in-law tried to lure him. "Your kids will study right here in your village and all of the village kids will become educated without going anywhere."

Hamid could not understand it; He usually did not understand things that were not directly beneficial to him.

"What will I get?" he asked without any foreword. "Is there any benefit to me or my family?"

"Yes, for you and your wife. My daughter will be offered a government job," his father-in-law played his triumph card.

"Ok, but she is not very educated. How can she get a teacher's job?" Hamid was little curious now.

"I have already arranged the solution for it. I have a friend who is a school teacher who will provide a class eighth certificate for her." His father-in-law was also a teacher in a Madrasa and had a lot of respect in the society.

"One more question." Hamid wanted his last doubt to be clarified. "She does not know how to read and write, she can't even sign her name. What would she teach the kids after becoming a teacher?"

"Don't worry my son-in-law. How many government teachers know how to teach? I have not met even one so far in my life. As far as the signature is concerned, it will take me half an hour to teach her how to sign it. After that, everything will be fine." his father-in-law clarified.

"But . . . but . . ." Hamid actually had nothing to say so he agreed.

After finishing lunch, he gave two small bags to them. It is actually a custom that whenever a father goes to meet a married daughter at her house, he usually carries some food items, which are grown in his own farm along with some other homemade food items. They took the bag and hid it behind the table. After that, talk continued.

"How's everything?" his father-in-law asked his daughter.

"Nothing is going well. I am very worried about Rani's marriage. Because she is handicapped, it will be very hard to find a right match for her. Who will marry her?" Rani's mother said all this in one go and then took a breath of relief.

"Don't worry my loving daughter! Allah is with you and everything will be solved soon insha Allah." he assured them as usual. "My nephew has three kids. The first one got married last year and the second one is very intelligent and religious. They want to have a relationship with our family but there is only one problem, which is that they don't have much money nor are they even landowners. They are hand-to-mouth people."

"Not a problem *baba*. I don't mind if they are poor people, but the thing is: will they accept Rani as their daughter-in-law because . . . ?"

"Leave it to me . . ." her father interrupted in between. "If you have no objections then I will talk to them further.

"We want to send Abid into a Madrasa so he can get a good education." She asked the last question of her father. "Do you know where we should send him?"

"Next week I will come and take him to a Madrasa. I know a better Madrasa for kids. The Madrasa where I teach is not for kids. It is only for adults. Make him ready to go next week. I will take him with me." The father-in-law came as a problem solver and gave solutions for everything.

"Ok, now I am going." Hamid's wife began crying. It was not because she had any reason to cry but because of the custom. He gave a one-rupee coin to every kid and went out. As soon as he left, the whole family surrounded the bag to check what it was.

They got some eatables and began falling on them to eat. Perhaps this was the reason she hid the bag until her father went.

From the next evening, the preparation began for Abid's departure to the Madrasa. Every evening, the women from the neighborhood had been called to beat rice. One woman takes one *musal* (threshing pestle) and another takes the other one. They pound with this into the wooden mortar called an *okhli* into which another woman had been deputed to put some rice. These women enjoyed it a lot. They also made some songs only for this occasion and they sang whenever they did this process. It continued every night for a week's time. In one week, they could collect a full bag of beaten rice, which is almost twenty-five kilos. When kids are sent to the Madrasa, they stay there continuously for a minimum of four to five months. There are some students who stay for a year or two. Madrasas provided them lunch and dinner free of cost but they had to manage their own breakfast. All of these preparations were done for their breakfast only. Guardians needed to give them enough soap, shampoo, toothpaste and other materials so that the children could be self-sufficient. For breakfast, beaten rice was prepared and the second item was *cesar*. *Cesar* is a tennis ball-size eatable, which is made of rice flour and sugar.

The next morning Hamid's father-in-law came to take him to the Madrasa. He had good news also for Hamid's family, which was that his cousin had agreed to come and see the girl formally for the engagement purpose.

"I fixed the appointment for this coming Tuesday. Hopefully everything will go well," he informed the family. "If the day is not good for you, then tell me and I will change the date."

"No, it's absolutely fine. Moreover, I am thrilled that everything is happening very quickly. *Ya* Allah! Please let everything go well!" Hamid could not control his happiness and thanked his father-in-law profusely.

The time came for Abid's departure. For Abid, this was his first time to leave his home so he was unable to understand what was actually going to happen to him. He called his grandfather *Nana*. He quietly went with his nana. On the carrier of a bicycle, the big bag of food had been tied tightly with a bicycle tube. In the handle a small bag was hung in which all the daily need stuff was put. The soap, shampoo, tooth paste etc. It was very hot sunny day so Abid's head was covered with a piece of cloth as they went towards their destination.

They reached the Madrasa where there was a big compound. In the middle of the compound, there was a hand pump. Two or three buckets were lying around, and some ten to twelve year old students were happily running around. As they saw Abid and his grandfather, they immediately understood that Abid was going to be a new student here.

Back in Hamid's house, engagement preparations were in full swing. The backside wall of the house had fallen down so the mason was immediately called to rebuild the wall because only one week remained before the event. Hamid had to order many things so he called the milkman and booked the order for milk. In order to clean the house, laborers had been called. Hamid called the people who rent out an electricity generator to arrange electricity for that specific day. Hamid had to invite all of the people who were near and dear to them. Because this was the first child's engagement in the family, socially, it was very important to have all of his brothers invited to this party.

Most of the main people of the village gathered in the evening at Hamid's house to ask about the preparations for the engagement. They discussed the arrangement for the reception of the guests along with who all was going to be invited to this prosperous occasion. It was a very old tradition of the village that whenever any function happened, they would all discuss arrangements and all kinds of preparation together. So, the villagers asked about whether he was going to invite his elder brother or not.

He kept quiet for a minute and went into deep thought then he asked the villagers what they would suggest, as they were already aware of what Rashid had done to him. The villagers talked together and reminded him that these occasions are very auspicious. They suggested that he forget all the previous hostility. Because you are the younger brother, you should go to him and seek forgiveness. Hamid's face became pale. Unwillingly he said yes because he was aware of the power of society. If he rejected their suggestions they would leave him alone and he wouldn't be able to do anything now or even in the future without their help and he would also not be invited to any special occasion in the village.

Chapter Three

That night was very difficult for him. He went to bed and did not talk to his wife. His wife understood that something was not right with him so she did not feel right asking him about anything. He went to bed and continued to think.

"He is the person who sent me to jail. We three brothers played together in our childhood. Since childhood, he has been trying to demoralize me. I never objected or uttered even a word in response but still he did not stop. He could not feel ashamed when I was sent to jail. Instead, he felt like he had won . . . How shameful it is . . . . I cannot go to him to invite him to the event. I know that I have a daughter but it does not mean that I don't have any self-respect. How can I go to him and tell him that I am sorry and say forgive me for my disobedience to you. He would laugh at me and tell me that he will think about it. No! I am not going to do this but I can't afford the villagers anger. What should I do?

How can I do this? I have to do so because I am a father of a daughter," he kept thinking.

He did not realize that his wife was right behind him and that she could feel his teardrops on her hand.

"Are you worried about inviting Rashid Mia?" she tried to share his pain.

"Hmm . . ."

"Don't worry! Allah will punish him for what he did." she said and wiped his tears gently.

"Why does Allah always favor him? Is he a saint?" he almost shouted angrily.

"He sent me to jail. What was my fault? He framed me only because of that! And now this society wants me to go to Rashid Mia and beg his grace . . . is this God's justice?" he disappointedly murmured and slept.

*

A *Maulana*, the Madrasa teacher, gave Abid two tasks. One was to memorize at least two pages from a book and the second task was to wash the Maulana's inner garments. Both of the tasks should be completed by sunset.

"Why did Maulana Sahib give me such a difficult task to do? Since my childhood, I have seen my mother washing my father's inner garment. Where is the Maulana's wife? She might have died," this little boy thought very seriously. "Maybe he has not married yet." Only after doing these things, could he memorize only one full page and a few lines of the second page. He was little bit afraid.

In the evening when the sunset and *Azan* was going on, the Maulana came, called Abid, and asked for a jar of water. He was very happy to see him because since his father left, the Maulana was the only person to whom he had been introduced. *Abba* had told him to follow each word the Maulana said. After finishing the prayer, the Maulana told him to come and recite the verses that he memorized and to bring the dried clothes. He was very nervous and could not utter a single word.

"Not a problem. This is your first day so go to bed but before that, make my bed and then enjoy your rest." Abid was very happy because he did not receive any punishment even though he could not finish the homework but as soon as he thought about his sister and he became sad that he was not there at home at her engagement. It was the happiest day of her life, and he was not there to celebrate. It was good that he was here away from Abba's everyday anger. He thought that Maulana Sahib was also a very good man. He loved him a lot, but he still had a question in his mind about why the Maulana let him wash his clothes. Maybe because of this only he loves him.

Someone came running and told Maulana that his wife wrote a letter to him. Maulana was very excited to read that letter.

"It means Maulana Sahib is a married man so why does he live alone?" Maybe there is no arrangement here to live with family or who knows, maybe it is not allowed in Islam." The small kid had much to think about. "It must be allowed in Islam to live with family because the Imam Sahib in the village lives with his wife and his three kids. Everyone in the village respects him, even Chand Mia who does not have a good reputation in the village. The next morning, the Maulana came early before the sunrise and brushed his hair to wake him gently. He woke up and the day started with the fixed routine of the Madrasa. Maulana Sahib had one pet goat that always waited for him. All of the students loved her a lot and fed her left over foods. Abid also liked to feed the goat. This Madrasa seemed to Abid to be a very good place to live. After a few hours, Abid got time to mix with the other Madrasa students and eat breakfast together. The beaten rice and *cesar* were very tasty according to other students as well. Every student of the Madrasa liked Abid because he was good in behavior. Moreover, he had some good food to share with them.

Chapter Four

Rani was a little nervous, sad and curious. She had many questions in her mind about her fiancé about his occupation, what he looks like, if he would love her and if his family would accept her or not?

In this period, they did not have the trend of exchanging photographs for two reasons. One reason was that getting a photo taken was not as easy as it is now and the second was that it was expensive too.

There was no option except thinking about him as a dream. Her friends began teasing her. She had nothing to reply. She used to hide her face in her palms whenever anyone talked about her fiancé. She neither saw him nor knew anything about him but she was planning to live her whole life with him because this was something in which there was a lot of happiness hidden. Her father, mother, and their relatives and friends all wanted this to happen.

The only thing she could do at this time was ask God for this engagement to be done without any obstacle.

There were many evil people in the society who wanted to break this engagement, because they were either detractors of their family or not well-wishers of her fiancé's family.

Hamid's father-in-law came, stood his bicycle on its stand, and came in. He looked a little bothered. As soon as he entered, Rani's mother almost ran to the hand pump with a steel glass in her hand, got the glass filled, came to him, and gave the glass to him with respect. She did not give it to him because he was her father but because he was the mediator of this new relationship. He came in and sat then put his hand on his forehead and showed himself very much worried.

"What happened?" Rani's father asked his father-in-law. "Is everything alright?"

"Actually, no" he replied with worry. "Someone is trying to break this relationship up."

"How can you say this?" they curiously asked.

"I talked to the boy's father yesterday and he was showing some doubts. He told me that he had heard that the girl is fully handicapped. I don't know who told him all that." he replied.

"What? Did you not tell them that Rani is handicapped?" Rani's parents surprisingly asked.

"Are you crazy? How could I have said that? If I had said that, they would never have agreed to this engagement?"

"It is wrong!"

"What's wrong in it? There is nothing wrong. It is called tactics."

"No, it's betrayal," Hamid decisively replied.

"If you carry this kind of principle then Rani will never get married. Who will marry her? It was not simple to arrange a suitable boy for her. I accomplished this task. You . . . . you are a fool. I am telling you that to arrange Rani's marriage won't be possible for you," his father-in-law warned him.

"But what will happen when they come to know the truth about Rani?" Rani's mother wanted to clear her doubt.

"I have a plan for this also." He shared his suggestion, "At the time of the engagement, she will be sitting in the middle of the house. At that time, all the guests will come but they will not enter in right at the time of coming. They will sit in the special guest room, which will be arranged temporarily for them. They will enter and complete the formality of the ring exchange. After that, the girl will not go inside but the guests will go outside for food. They will never know that she is handicapped. It's very simple," the father-in-law shared his idea. By sharing his idea, he was showing himself, as he was the wisest person in the world.

"But, after the marriage, they will come to know about her disability. Then what will we do?" she asked the last question to be clarified. Hamid did not let his father-in-law speak. "No ifs ands or buts. Once the marriage is over then no one will do anything. After all, they are our relatives."

"But the problem is still there. I don't know who is trying to break this relationship up. If he tells the truth to the boy's family then this engagement will not take place and then even I won't be able to fix this problem. I hope they will not listen to them." He seemed worried.

"Insha Allah everything will be alright. Allah is merciful. We should not waste time here. We should finish all the preparations by tomorrow so that the day after tomorrow, the engagement will be done."

Outside of Hamid's house was a big piece of land. They tied ropes every two feet on all four sides of the house, hung them over and stuck colorful papers of all seven colors on the ropes. This was not an easy task so it took five people all day to do it. Finally, it looked like an engagement was going to happen in the house. People started asking about the decorations and had many questions like, "What is going to happen? Who is getting engaged? Etc." Hamid replied proudly to everybody that his daughter was getting engaged. They bought three suits for Rani's fiancé. The suits were little expensive but nothing was more valuable than Rani's happiness.

"Rani was lying on the bed. No one asked her what she wanted because everyone knew that she was a good girl and she would certainly be happy because her parents were happy. That was true. She was happy. Maybe because she wanted her parents to be happy, possibly, she did not have any other choice, or she was happy because every girl has this dream of her life, including her.

The next morning, she had traditional *mehndi* put on her palms. Her friends and a few other women sat around her and sang traditional songs that say, "From tomorrow onward my daughter won't be free anymore and she will no longer be our family member. She will be a guest who will go back to her home. She will become a guest to us."

Her cheeks were wet with tears, not because she was sad but because of she knew that very soon this home would not be more than a relative's house for her and that she would become a member of a family she didn't know anything about. Rani did not know whether she was happy or sad but one thing she was pretty sure about was that her parents would certainly be very happy after finishing this task.

She kept thinking about her new home where she was going to go as bride. She was mature enough to understand that in the new home she would have to carry many duties which she may like or dislike. Willingly or unwillingly, she would have to play all the roles as a new member of a new family. She was a little afraid at the same time. Her fear was whether or not they would accept a handicapped girl as their family member. She did not know whether her would-be fiancée's family knew anything about her or not. Her parents hid her disability from the boy's family.

In the afternoon time, Hamid's father-in-law came. He was almost gasping. He carried very bad news that the boy's family was not coming for the engagement because the boy's father was suffering from fever.

"How's that possible? You are lying!" Hamid's father said.

"No, I'm serious. It's true, but I don't think his father has a fever. The reason is certainly different. He has come to know that Rani is handicapped. Someone may have told him . . . . just guessing." He assured them that he was not joking.

This was the first time Rani heard that her parents hid the truth from them. She was shocked. She had never expected that her parents could be liars.

Because of the engagement being broke, the phenomenon turned into mourning. Everyone in the family was sad. Thus, few of them pretended that they were not happy but actually, they were happy inside because they were not the friends in need.

The colorful papers were flapping in the air. The colors of the colorful paintings on the wall had lost their brightness but they were still there. Rani's mother was sitting alone in the room. She was confused about what she should do. Hamid was getting angry at everything and every person. Hamid's father-in-law was busy figuring out who the person could be who played the role in breaking up this relationship and why. In anger, Hamid did not care about his father-in-law's respect and he used many swear words at him. As a result of that, he met his daughter, Rani's mother, and told her very clearly that he would not try to offer any help for Rani's marriage ever again in the future but he would continue coming every week or two to see her because she was his daughter.

Rani had nothing about which to dream. Her father had no hope now. Her mother was a little more worried because she could not figure out how she would give this information to Rani and what Rani's reaction would be. Moreover, the family had spent a lot of money for this expected engagement and this all went astray.

Chapter Five

Abid was very happy now. He had started dreaming that very soon he would finish his education and become like his grandfather, the respected and prestigious personality of the whole village. No more would they call me a notorious boy, they will call me with respect. About sunset, after the evening prayer called *Maghreb*, he was sitting on the roof and memorizing the verses of the Quran with his other friends when he looked up into the sky. It was full of stars. The twinkling stars reminded him that today his most loving elder sister was getting engaged and poor he could not be there. However, this was not a problem. Everyone would be at home and would be very happy. The celebration will make my father and mother happy and it would let his father forget the jail incident.

While he was pondering all that, he realized that he did not memorize his lesson tonight. He started memorizing the verses but he could not finish it and time was up. He took his plates and cups, washed them and stood in the cue for dinner. A very fat man was sitting on a little high seat cooking *Tanddori Roti,* a kind of bread, of which he would give two to every child. A person who had a long beard sat before a giant pot from which he took one spoon of beef and one spoon of gravy and he would pour it on the student's plate. Whomsoever he liked the most, he would give half a spoon more. It was given not because of his good behavior but because of his good looks. Abid was also very cute so he got half a spoon extra and he was very happy.

He was about to finish his dinner when suddenly he heard a big noise on the grounds outside of the mosque on the campus of the Madrasa. He saw people running towards the grounds so he also ran to see what happened. He reached the crowd and heard a child yelling and crying. A Maulana who had a thin long stick in his hand was shouting at him. He was very angry. Abid came to know that he did not memorize his lesson so the Maulana was beating him very bitterly. Abid was stunned and stood there like a statue. The Maulana moved to the crowd of students, scolded them and ordered them to go from there.

Abid came back to kitchen to finish the rest of his food. Two elder kids came in the corner and began talking to each other.

"Mumtaz is a very cute boy. Why did the Maulana beat him so badly? If he did not memorize his lesson it is not that a big mistake." one kid said to another with curiosity.

"The lesson is not the matter." He called the first kid closer to say something in his ear. Abid was also very curious to know so he also stayed close. "He did not go to the Maulana's bed to serve him last night even though the Maulana called him many times," the other kid laughed. "Did you not see how rigorously the Maulana was beating him? It is not good. The Maulana should not have beaten him so ruthlessly."

"Who can stop him?" the other kid asked. "No one," he answered himself.

This was Abid's first bitter experience in the Madrasa. Thanks to Allah that his Maulana was not that way. He was very nice to him. He thought and then went to bed.

"What if it happens to me? I will not be able to tolerate it." Abid was thinking.

"If it happens to me I will run away," he said to himself.

He was in the bed. He thought about his home and his sister and he tried to feel the happiness as he thought it would be in his home. He did not know the reality but he thought everybody at home would be happy and excited about Rani.

"I will go home for her marriage at any cost," he promised himself. "This time no one will be able to stop me. Not this Maulana, not my father, not anyone." He was in deep thought so he did not realize when he fell asleep.

A boy came in the room and woke him up with a jolt. "Wake up Abid! Wake up! Maulana Sahib is calling you to his room." he said and went to his bed.

Abid unwillingly woke up and went to the room where the Maulana was lying in the bed. Abid sat down on the mat near his teacher's bed.

The Maulana turned the light on and told Abid to bring his book and read the memorized lesson. Abid hesitantly brought the book and read one page. The

Maulana's behavior was not normal. He told Abid to memorize the complete lesson immediately. Abid was a little upset because he was feeling sleepy. He went outside, washed his face, came back in and told Abid to wash his face as well so he wouldn't feel drowsy.

"Not a problem. You can memorize it later." The Maulana began the talk showing a little bit of friendliness.

"Do you like this Madrasa?" he asked.

"Yes but . . ." He was hesitant to share.

"Tell me if you have any problems," the Maulana said to him being a little friendly with Abid.

"Today I saw that Maulana Sahib was brutally beating a student named Mumtaz. I was afraid." he finally shared his feeling.

"Don't worry. It won't happen to you." the Maulana said to him and called him up on the bed pointing with his finger.

Abid came to the bed and began tapping the teacher's feet. Tapping a teacher's feet is a part of traditional Madrasa culture, though it's not a religious thing to do. The conversation was going on and Maulana was touching Abid's cheeks more frequently. That was making Abid a bit uncomfortable but the Maulana continued to rub his cheeks.

Then, Maulana Sahib turned off the light.

After a few minutes, Abid ran out to the field yelling and crying. Maulana came out following him and caught him with his arm and warned him that if he did not want to be beaten, as Mumtaz, then he should come back quickly to his room otherwise he should remember that he hadn't memorized his lessons yet either.

Abid sat on a chair that was lying outside and began planning what he should do. He thought to tell everything to his father but after a few minutes, he recalled what his father told him on the way to the Madrasa. It seemed to Abid that his father had a lot of respect toward this Maulana so he might not believe what Abid would tell him. It was very cold and dark outside. Finally, he decided to go back to the Maulana's room and he was mentally prepared to run away from the Madrasa the next morning.

He came to the room where the teacher was waiting for him. Maulana Sahib also understood that this boy was not going to agree to what he wanted.

"Don't discuss this incidence with anyone in this Madrasa. Otherwise, you know well what happened to Mumtaz. I like you very much so I will not treat you like him but remember that if you tell about anybody, I will not be nice to you. I will screw your happiness so don't talk about it, not even with your father." Maulana warned him in order to hide this incident, which could spoil his reputation.

Abid nodded his head in agreement and went to bed. The next morning he behaved normally with everybody like nothing happened.

He woke up early in the morning, washed his face, hands and feet and went to the mosque for the morning worship. The Maulana was *Imam* for that prayer and he led the prayer. After finishing the prayer, he took his book and went to the class to memorize the rest of the lessons. The other students were talking about him and when they saw Abid, they stopped talking. Abid noticed it.

"How was the night with Maulana?" one of them asked Abid and laughed.

"You shut up," he replied and started reading the Quran. Other students were talking and rocking themselves back and forth to pretend like they were busy memorizing their lessons.

Chapter Six

All the guests were now gone from Hamid's home. Hamid and his wife were sitting at the door outside where Hamid's elder brother Rashid and a few other villagers were discussing what had happened in the last two days.

"Whatever Allah does is to our benefit," one of the villagers said.

"Yes, you are right. If they rejected your daughter that is not too bad, think about what if it had happened after marriage?" The other villager showed sympathy to Hamid.

"I have a chance to attend one more feast. I will come back to the next engagement. God bless you my brother." Rashid said with a sarcastic smile and went back home.

Hamid felt very bad but did not say anything because he always paid him respect when he was with him.

One by one everyone left. Only three people were sitting at Hamid's House: Hamid, his wife and Rani.

Hamid and his wife started talking about paying the bills for the decorations and the other labor charges. Actually, they were only wastage of money. Hamid was very worried now about Rani's marriage.

"Who will marry this lame girl? Why did God give me this tribulation? I always earned money with hard work. Why does God not give this kind of tribulation to the people who cheat and become rich? They don't get a handicapped child. Their children are usually fit and beautiful." He was in deep thought. "Not a problem. One day, my son will finish his study in the Madrasa, he will be able to get a good job, and then people will come to me to marry my son. At that time, I will also ask them whether they have a healthy daughter or not." A teardrop fell on his hand.

"Look who is coming!" Rani's mother shouted with joy. "It's Abid. He is coming. As soon as Rani heard it, she became very happy like a kid.

"His father was not happy but he was a little curious to know why he came from the Madrasa and what might have happened."

"Why did you come from the Madrasa? What happened?" he asked.

"Nothing happened." Abid said with anger, put his bag down and looked at Rani.

"Rani your engagement has been done now. After a few months, you will get married then I will come to your home and your husband will welcome me there. I will also stay with you because nobody will be there to scold me." Rani eyes became red and watery.

"Yes," she said.

Abid looked at his mother and father's faces and understood that something was wrong here because no one was happy.

"But why did you come?" Hamid asked again.

"Can't you see that he walked a long way with this heavy bag? Let him relax. He is tired now. You can ask your questions later." his mother interfered.

Abid hugged and kissed his mother and went to the bathroom.

"But at least he should tell me that what happened." Hamid was a little displeased with his wife's behavior.

That night at dinner, Hamid again asked Abid with love about what happened in the Madrasa and why he came.

"I don't want to study in the Madrasa anymore," he gave his decision to his parents.

"But why is that so?" his mother asked him.

"I said I don't want to study and I don't think I have to tell you why. I am not going to go to that Madrasa. This is my decision." he explained but did not give any reason.

At this time, his father became angry, took out his stick and hit him. He began crying and yelling.

"I will not go to the Madrasa even if you kill me," Abid shouted.

"Then you will have to come with me every day to the field and farm with me. Do you agree?" Hamid's voice was loud and he was very angry at this time.

"Yes," Abid replied and agreed to do the farming.

"Is this your final decision that you don't want to study further?" Hamid asked.

"Yes," Abid replied.

"I had a lot of hope for you but you made it all in vain. Not a problem. Jawed will go to the Madrasa and he will study and do something to change our lifestyle.

It was late at night so they all went to bed. Rani had done her duty of making beds for all family members and then went to her bed. Abid was tired from walking so he slept also. Hamid was very upset so he could not sleep even though he was trying to sleep.

"I am thinking about sending Rani to school. Because of her broken engagement she will not be feeling good. If she would go to school and talk to her friends she would feel better." Rani's mother suggested to her father.

"Are you crazy? Here I am worried about her marriage and you are planning for her study. Remember even after studying and having a good job she is not going to give you anything. Whatever she earns, will be her husband's money not yours so why do you want to spend on her education? If you want to think, think about her marriage. That will solve your problem. Next time, please do not talk nonsense with me. Abid is a boy. If he studies then whatever he earns he will give to me. That will be our income." Hamid said very clearly to her.

"I am not a businessman who always thinks about profit and loss like you. I am a mother who wants her children to grow in life." She began weeping. They all slept after a few minutes. They were all very tired.

Chapter Seven

Hamid had to think about his daughter's marriage, farming, and raising Abid and Jawed with love. These things could not make him forget the mosquito sting and darkness in the jail and that scary night. He could only stake his agenda of revenge behind his responsibility. Whenever he remembered that night, he started shaking with anger. Arranging Rani's marriage was his need but the revenge was his prime motivation. His wife was a bit worried about his this tendency of thinking about revenge, so most of the time, when he became angry she had to cool him off. His wife wanted him to be worried about Rani's marriage and not to focus on revenge because she knew that revenge was not going to benefit the family. Besides this, she was a mother as well so obviously the settlement of her children was her priority.

Hamid and his wife both wanted Rani's marriage but they were unable to think of a way to get a boy who would marry their handicapped girl. By then Rani had come to know that her marriage was not an easy task for her parents. She had already killed all her dreams of being a princess daughter-in-law of someone's house. Now, she did not have big hopes about her new family.

Hamid and his wife were both sitting outside under the tree and they were busy thinking about Rani's marriage. The Maulana of the Madrasa where Abid had been sent to study came by bicycle and stood there. Abid was scared. He thought that the Maulana would ask his father and him to send him to the Madrasa once again. He ran away. The Maulana came.

"Assalam-o-Alaikum."

"Walaikum Assalam."

"How are you Hamid Sahib? Is everything alright?"

"Yes, everything is fine. But . . ." Hamid answered with sorrow.

"What is the problem Hamid Sahib? You are a respected person of this village. Please tell me if you have any trouble. You are like my father. Please tell me so that maybe I can help you." He offered his help.

"Maulana Sahib! As you know, Rani is my daughter and her situation is not hidden from you. She is a handicapped girl. Who will marry a lame girl? As you know, I don't have much money. This is the problem I have, but I know there is nothing we can do about it. Please pray for our family." Hamid said, having in his mind that he wouldn't be able to help him.

"I have one person in mind who may agree to marry your daughter if you agree to this relationship and allow me to talk further. He is a son of your wife's cousin. He is very religious. You might be wondering why he would marry while he knows that the girl is handicapped. Let me tell you the truth. The boy is more than thirty years old and he is eager to marry. Because he is an older guy, no one will marry him. He has a beard, he wears a cap, and he prays five times a day. I mean to say that his family is good and religious." Maulana Sahib said.

"But why did he not get married yet?" Hamid's wife asked with curiosity.

"Because the family was looking for a religious girl and they could not find one in the Syed caste. I think they would like your daughter because she is religious." Maulana Sahib explained.

"That will be great. Will they demand a dowry?" Hamid asked.

"I don't think so but if you allow me, I can tell them about this proposal and find out about the dowry." he replied.

"Yes, of course you should proceed." Hamid and his wife both said with eagerness.

"Would you like to drink some tea or coffee?" they added.

"No thanks. Maybe next time." Maulana said and went from there happily.

Abid was afraid and hiding behind the tree. When he saw Maulana Sahib going, he came out. He was a little scared to think that his parents were going to scold him because certainly Maulana Sahib would have said something bad about him. However, the case was completely different.

"Abid! Where are you going son? Come here!" He heard the voice and stood stunned.

"What did Maulana Sahib say? Did he talk about me?" Abid asked with fear.

"No, absolutely not. He was trying to arrange a marriage for Rani. He is a very good person." Abid's mother told Abid.

"Yes, surely he is." Abid said sarcastically. However, his mother could not understand the sarcasm behind his tone and said yes.

The next day, Maulana Sahib came again with good news. He told them they agreed but they would like to see the girl before the marriage.

"Sure. Why not?" was the answer of Hamid and his wife. "But we don't want an engagement ceremony. If they like Rani, then we will set the date of marriage." Hamid said.

"Wow, what a coincidence! They also want the same thing."

"What does the boy do?"

"He runs a medical shop owned by his father. There are three brothers. The eldest one married a year ago and they are going to have a baby very soon." Maulana Sahib informed them.

"That's great!"

"Can you tell us little more about that family?" Hamid's wife asked further.

"Their father used to be a landlord in Rampur but at the time of partition of the country, he decided to shift to Pakistan. After living for twenty years in Pakistan, he missed his homeland a lot and finally decided to come back. The boy was born there only. However, when they came back, they had already lost their lands. The neighbors and relatives captured all of their properties and they were not ready to give them back. Therefore, the boy's mother offered a piece of land to build a house and live there. He worked very hard to settle himself here but his wife, the boy's mother, died so he had to remarry. He married a girl who had some property. She sold some of the property and gave them a medical store to run to support them. So now he takes other people's land on contract to farm and their kids run the store." Maulana Sahib added more information.

Chapter Eight

The boy, whose proposal of marriage with Rani was under consideration, was named Reza. He had one elder brother named Mujeeb, a younger brother named Rizwan, a stepmother named Atia, and a father, Dr. Syed. Villagers used to call Dr. Syed Doctor Sahib. Doctor Sahib did not have any medical or PhD degrees. Because he worked as an assistant with several physicians in the past, he had some knowledge of treatment for a few health complaints. His knowledge about medicine led him to open a medical store for his son with the help of his second wife's money. Doctor Sahib used to help villagers with their health complaints. Doctor Sahib strongly believed in practicing Islam and the teachings of Islam so he never cheated anybody in his entire life, although sometimes he had been cheated by other people around him. After returning from Pakistan, he loved his villagers, relatives and friends more than he used to. He experienced many ups and downs in his life. His father passed away when he was a small kid. His mother was a teacher. She raised him up with lots of love and care. From their forefathers they inherited many big pieces of land and his family was quite a strong family. They were considered a wealthy family in the society. However, because of his decision of migrating from the country, he lost everything. Because he had a strong educated family background, he always tried to educate his family but because of his struggles in his life, he could not give them formal education for more than class tenth. However, he always taught them the value of education so they were involved in earning bread and butter and they always tried to get an education.

Doctor Sahib had a smiling face, big eyes and a long white beard. He always wore a cap. He prayed five times a day without fail. He attended and participated in religious meetings at regular intervals.

His sons had also inherited good values from him, especially Reza. Though Mujeeb wanted to cross all the limits in order to earn money, he never did cross his limits. Rizwan did not have much opportunity to live with his father so he did not learn much about values. He was socially very active. All three brothers had different duties to bear according to their interests and choices. Rizwan used to take care of farming and cultivation related works and Reza took care of the shop and related matters. These three brothers had started a school for minorities. Mujeeb worked hard to affiliate it by the state government so most of the time he was out in the district town for this business.

Doctor Sahib preferred his son's' career to their marriages so it took a long time. Since he did not find his sons future settlement up to his expectations, he decided to arrange their marriages but he had to work hard to arrange his son's marriages because they had become older than the age of marriage. For Reza, he could not find a better match than Rani. Moreover, it would be a work of charity and ritual because she was a handicapped girl. He discussed this proposal with his sons and finally he agreed to it.

He did not want to spend a lot of money on the marriage for two reasons. One was he did not have money to waste and the second reason was that wasting money is prohibited in Islam.

He went to Hamid's home with Maulana Sahib. Hamid's wife was his cousin so he did not have many things to inquire about.

"I would like to do this noble event in the mosque without any unnecessary expenses." Doctor Sahib said to Hamid's wife.

"We do not want to waste a penny either. We would like to accomplish this task simply as well but I want a few villagers and all my brothers to attend this ceremony." Hamid spoke on her behalf.

"Ok, then we will fix a date for marriage and you will come with not more than ten people including your near and dear ones. The *Nikah* will be done by Maulana Sahib in the mosque here and after that, we will organize a feast in which you will participate. After that, Rani will go to your house and will become your family member forever." Hamid's wife suggested.

While this meeting was going on, Rashid was curious about what was happening at Hamid's house so he came by and when he saw Doctor Sahib he came in and greeted him warmly.

"How are you Doctor Sahib? Long time no see." Rashid said for nicety and in curiosity about what was going there.

"It is good that your elder brother also came. Nothing can be finalized without his consideration." Doctor Sahib said being generous with him. He told Rashid everything about the meeting. Rashid smiled and did not say anything.

"Brother, what would be a good date in your opinion?" Hamid asked him gently.

"What do you think?"

"We have not decided yet."

"What about Thursday after fifteen days from now and we will do *Walima* (the feast) on Friday?"

"That is a good idea," Doctor Sahib agreed happily.

"OK, then it is final now. What do you say Hamid?" Rashid asked.

"I agree with whatever you decide," Hamid said gently.

"Did you ask your son Reza about this new relationship Doctor Sahib?" Rashid asked to find out whether everyone was in agreement with this relation or not. "I mean to ask: does he know about Rani?" Rashid added.

"Who is he to think of all this? I am his father. I know the good and bad things about him, of course whatever I say he will agree with me. So far, he has never said any if, and, or but about my decisions.

"That's good then."

"Hamid get some sweets. Rani's marriage has been fixed now." Rashid ordered Hamid without showing off that there are no differences among them. It was a social need also because no one likes a family with differences so they never let others know about what's going on among them in front of outsiders.

Hamid called Abid. He came with the fear he still had in his mind that Maulana Sahib would complain about him to his father. However, when he saw his father smiling and happy (which rarely happened) he felt a little relieved. "Go and get two kilos of *laddu*." He ordered Abid. Laddu is a sweet, famous for giving good news. It did not take long for Abid to understand that some good news was there. Then laddu was distributed in the village.

After fifteen days, the marriage happened. It was not much fun for Rani because she was so disappointed that it was hard for her to believe that she was getting married.

For Hamid, it was a great thing because his biggest burden of responsibility was going to be taken away for forever. His only wish was to finish the task somehow with dignity.

Whenever he saw Rashid, his wound turned unhealed, He could not forget the terrible night in the jail. Once this marriage was accomplished without any obstacle, then he would plan for his revenge. This was his agenda.

All Rani's childhood friends were there with her. They teased her and tried to make her happy but she was content and she did not respond to them. It seemed like she realized now that this was her last day with them and from now onward, she was going to have a different life. She did not have any dreams of a prince who would come on a horse and take her with him for forever like the one she heard in the children's stories. She wanted to be alone and sit in peace. She wanted to talk to her mother but she was very busy and she wanted to see her father. She had many questions to ask her parents like why would a girl like her in the society be given this punishment where she gets lots of love from her parents and suddenly she has to leave her home, parents and brothers and sister? Why did she have to go to a new family where a brand new mother father and other members would welcome her where she would have to manage herself willingly or unwillingly to live with them? What if she did not like the new family or they did not like her? She knew the answer was that a girl could not afford not to like her new family. Even if the new family didn't like her, she still had to adjust with them somehow. This is a girl's destiny in India. She had to bury these questions in her heart. However, mother is a mother. She could easily read what a child thinks by the child's face. She could understand the feeling very quickly and why not? She also went through this process. She took Rani's face in her hands and looked in her eyes, which were filled with tears. Neither talked but understood the each other's feelings.

Traditionally, seven days before the date of marriage, the women, relatives and friends of the bride gather at bride's home. They sing the traditional songs and apply *ubtan* to bride's face and body to make her look brighter. *Ubtan* is a homemade beauty pack made out of herbs like turmeric, oil, mustard and other ingredients. Meanwhile they tease the bride about her marriage and sometimes they make fun of the groom also but no one takes it as an offence. It happened with Rani as well. The bride was stopped from doing any physical work at home. The same goes for the groom at his house as well. Rani was neither very happy nor very sad about her marriage.

Reza was very excited about his marriage. He knew that the girl he was going to marry was a handicapped girl but still he was very happy to meet his bride. Culturally, it was not possible for him to see the girl before marriage.

He could not meet his life partner but he could manage to see the young and beautiful girl named Leila, the younger sister of Rani. She was very beautiful. Rani would certainly be a very beautiful lady because her younger sister was pretty, he guessed. Because of extreme Islamic custom, there was no tradition of exchanging photographs in those days. Things have changed nowadays.

The groom and his companion arrived at Rani's house where Rani's father and his elder brother welcomed the *barat* with *sharbat* (a kind of sweet drink). Barat is an Urdu word, which means a group of people. The word is especially used for groom's companions in marriage ceremonies. The groom's face was covered with a thin transparent cloth and flowers called *sehra*. He wore white kurta and pajama. After having a small breakfast, most of the villagers were called to the mosque for attending the ceremony of *nikah*. Nikah is a formal wedding process. After the Maulana pronounced the nikah speech in Arabic, he asked the groom, "Do you accept?" The groom said, "I accept" and then everybody raised hands for prayer. After the prayer, people ran to the groom to congratulate him and Hamid as well.

The barat stayed in the bride's village all night in a camp and the next day the groom was ready to take the bride with them. Every woman at home suddenly began crying and hugging Rani one by one. This was actually part of the tradition. Rani's mother was actually crying because she knew that her daughter was leaving home for forever and from now onward, she would not be a member of this family anymore.

A tall man with a short beard came to the front, hugged Doctor Sahib, and greeted him warmly. Doctor Sahib was a bit surprised because this was the same person who came by one day, and told him bad things about Hamid. He told him about how bad Hamid was and how badly they (both brothers) fought with each other. Moreover, the man went to Hamid and met with him also as he is his very good friend as well. Hamid invited him to attend the marriage party. He was none other than Chand Mia.

Doctor Sahib called Hamid and started talking to him.

"Who is this tall man?"

"He is Chand Mia. He is Rashid's friend."

"O . . . hmm . . ."

"What happened?"

"Nothing . . . He came to me a long time ago and tried to convince me not to agree to this marriage. I did not listen to him."

"Hmm . . . He is the kind of a person who does not become happy when happiness knocks on anyone's door." Hamid said.

"I know that. I did not listen to him but I was just wondering who invited him here."

"I did not invite him," Hamid said.

"I did not invite him either." Doctor Sahib clarified.

Chand Mia came suddenly and interrupted them. "What are you both talking about?" he asked.

"Nothing. We were just thinking that everything has been done now without any difficulty." Hamid tried to hide.

"That's true, "Chand Mia said." I thought you might be wondering about what a surprise it was that I came here. So let me tell you. Actually, your elder brother Rashid, who is a good friend of mine, invited me for his niece's marriage. I know that you were thinking that you were too busy to invite me but don't worry, I am not displeased at all with either of you. I know that in marriage there is a lot of work so it is hard to keep everyone in mind and I am like your family member. And, in fact, there is no need to invite a family member, is there?" Chand Mia talked very friendly.

"You are right." Doctor Sahib said for curtsey.

"In fact, family members have the right to invite others. They do not need an invitation." Hamid added.

"This is the reason that I invited someone here and I know that you won't have any objections. Am I right?" Chand Mia asked both of them. Both stood stunned because they knew that he was certainly going to create some troubles.

"Sir, please come here." he called someone from the crowd.

A man, in white kurta pajamas, came out from among the guests. He was very fat and he had a scary mustache. His mouth was full of *paan* and as he came closer, he spat paan on the wall rudely and in a misbehaving way. When he came closer, Hamid could recognize him very easily. He was the same police officer who took him to jail and tortured him in the jail very ruthlessly. He was very frightening to Hamid.

Before Hamid could say anything, he said, "Don't be afraid. I did not come here to take you to jail. Actually, Chand Mia is my very good friend. He told me that his niece was getting married and told me that you are her father. Then I thought I should come to meet you and bless your daughter. O, Doctor Sahib! How are you? You are our guest. If you have any trouble, you can tell me I will fix it. I am a police officer of this area but I came here in civil dress because I wanted to attend this marriage party. Hamid is a good friend of mine." The police officer said all this in one go without any pause.

Hamid felt very insulted but he could not say anything because inside he was feeling like somebody slapped him in public.

"This Chand Mia is completely unmannered. What was the need of calling that police officer Ram Pathak to this marriage ceremony? I should not have invited this stupid Chand Mia." Rashid whispered in Hamid's ear and looked in Hamid's eyes, smiled sarcastically and moved away from there. Hamid felt like someone rubbed salt on his wound.

His attitude of revenge, which was almost gone, emerged again. He looked at Rashid with anger.

The barat was packing up to go back. The women got the bride ready to go. Chand Mia and Ram Pathak were sitting in the corner drinking tea. Chand Mia called Hamid and asked, "Why don't you compromise with Rashid? The fight will not give you any benefit. Do one thing: give that piece of land to Rashid, which he claimed belongs to him. It is not wise to go to jail repeatedly for that small piece of land. Nowadays, the legal fight is very costly. It will cost you more than the land is worth. What do you say?"

"I will think about it." Hamid said and became busy in arranging the return of the barat. After a few minutes, Rashid came to them and asked Ram Pathak, "What happened?"

"Nothing yet." Chand Mia replied on his behalf.

Finally, the barat was ready to leave. Doctor Sahib, Reza, the groom, Mujeeb, the elder brother of the groom, and Rizwan all came to Hamid and his family to tell them good-bye. They shook hands one-by-one with everybody including Rashid, Ram Pathak and Chand Mia.

When Hamid saw his daughter in bridal suit, he could not stop his eyes from filling with tears. Hamid's wife, Abid, Leila, Jawed and all Rani's sisters were sad and waving to Rani, told her good-bye and prayed for her to have a good marital life.

Rani was happy and sad at the same time. She was happy because she got married and sad because she was leaving behind the family she had lived with all her life.

Chapter Nine

When the barat returned to Kazinagar, Rani went down to her new home where the relatives and family members of Reza welcomed her warmly. Doctor Sahib became busy in distributing sweets among the villagers. Rani was sent to her bedroom to rest. Though the distance between Kazinagar and Rani's village was not much, only around twenty kilometers, she still was very tired.

The next morning, Mujeeb and Doctor Sahib called Reza into the drawing room, which was made of grass. Doctor Sahib addressed all three sons there in general and Reza in particular.

"We live happily in our family. This is a tradition in the village that whenever a woman comes into the family, she always tries to break the bonding of the brotherhood. So, try to be committed and don't listen to your wife if she talks about anything that may become the reason of enmity in the family. I would like to see all three of you always united together. If you stay united, you will be able to win any battle in your life. So remember, don't let anyone break your family. In the future if any dispute happens, then all three of you should sit together and try to solve it. Is that clear to you all?" he asked. All three brothers said yes to him.

After that, Doctor Sahib called all three brothers inside the house as well as both women, Shakko, the wife of Mujeeb and Rani and said, "Whenever two women stay together they always clash but if they sacrifice for each other then they live together with comfort."

Both women were sitting there covered and turning down their heads in respect. It was village culture not to utter a word when the head of the family speaks. They abided by this, did not say anything, and agreed to everything that Doctor Sahib said to them. "You can divide the indoor duty, for example. Shakko can do all the cleaning and Rani can be responsible for cooking related jobs, vice-versa, or whatever way you would like. It's all up to you. However, Shakko is pregnant so for now, Rani should do as much as possible and she ought to give full attention to taking care of the needs of Shakko. Do you agree?" Doctor Sahib politely asked Rani.

"Yes Mamu." Rani agreed to him.

Rani used to call her father-in-law *Mamu* because he was her mother's cousin.

Because Rani was handicapped, it was difficult for her to sweep the floor completely but she always did it nicely. She had a habit of working hard at home because she had done it all at her mother's house. She used to wake up early in the morning when then dawn would say good-bye to the night. Before any of the family members awoke, she used to finish cleaning and dusting and start cooking breakfast. When the other family members woke up, they would see her cooking. She would get breakfast ready then she would take a plate for Shakko to her room. Then she would clean utensils, cook lunch and dinner, and so on. She would be very tired by sunset. This routine went on until Shakko gave birth to a cute baby boy.

The time when the child was born everyone was happy at home. Rani also became pregnant. Everybody at home was happy because Mujeeb was the father of the baby. When they came to know about Rani's pregnancy, they had a good surprise. The disease Rani was suffering from was Poliomyelitis. In that case, chances of pregnancy are usually very slim. When Hamid and his wife heard this news, they were very excited and planned to see their daughter. They both came to see her and congratulated her and her family.

Now she was pregnant so she was unable to do the routine work of home. Because she helped Shakko a lot when she was pregnant, this was her turn to be paid back. However, she did not get her expectations fulfilled. She had to do all the routine work and on top of that, she had to take care of herself as well.

One day, she tried to share her problem with her husband but he was not ready to listen to her because he had his father's admonition in his mind that woman always try to break the unity of the family.

"One kilo of milk comes into the home for you and the baby. I think it is sufficient to feed you and my nephew." Reza said to Rani.

"I swear I did not get even a single sip of that. Shakko takes all the milk for herself and her baby." Rani said with sorrow.

"Don't tell me this. I don't trust you. Why would my sister-in-law do this? She is not unjust." Reza replied.

"Then what do you mean the one kilo of milk that child drinks only?" told Rani.

"Do not ever try to break our relationship! We are a family and we will always be a family. This kind of stupid complaint may break our unity and none of us wants this to happen. Do you get it?" Reza warned her and left.

Shakko, stealthily, heard their conversation and told her husband Mujeeb but she told only one side of the story. She did not tell him what she did.

Mujeeb came out of the room and went to the men's room outside. They were all sitting for lunch. Mujeeb was very angry and he was waiting for Reza to begin the conversation about the whole scenario.

Reza was a little frustrated about what his wife said to him but he forgot it after a while. He remembered that the monthly rent of the shop was due for this month so he needed to know wether he needed to pay it tomorrow on thirtieth or whether he needed to wait until the seventh of the next month.

At dinnertime, he said to Mujeeb, "I want to talk to you about something important." Reza wanted to talk about the rent.

"I know what you want to talk about. You want to talk about that which your wife convinced you. You want to talk about why my wife drinks the milk and why she doesn't give the milk to the little kid. Right? I know what your wife wants and why. One thing that is very clear is that she does not like my child. She hates him because she does not have her own baby yet." Mujeeb said all that without a pause. He was very angry.

"No, there is nothing like that brother . . ." before Reza completed his sentence Mujeeb again angrily started saying, "If you think that you are the only person in the family earning money then you are wrong. It's true that you sit in the shop but it does not mean that I don't do anything or that Rizwan does not do anything. Everybody in the house has the same rights. No less and no more, ok?" Mujeeb almost scolded Reza.

Reza was a little upset because this was the first time that his brother so angry. He thought that his wife must've said something to either his elder brother, Mujeeb, or to his brother-in-law that made him so angry. He was just wondering. Rizwan also did not talk to him as friendly as he used to do.

Reza entered in his room. His wife was resting after cleaning and cooking. Outside of the room in the corner of the courtyard, there was a kitchen where Shakko was busy cleaning the dishes.

"Did you eat something?" Reza asked.

"No."

"Why?"

"There is nothing left in the kitchen."

"What? Why there is nothing in the kitchen?"

"I don't know." Rani was a bit harsh in her tone.

Reza could not figure out what to say. He just stayed calm and went to bed. Late at night, Doctor Sahib came back from where he had been for his work.

The next morning at breakfast, he asked his sons, "Is everything all right?"

"Yes," Reza said.

"Nothing is all right." Rizwan replied.

"What happened?" Doctor Sahib inquired.

"Hmm . . . The new family member started sowing the seed of hatred among us." Mujeeb said. In addition, she is convincing Reza that my wife does not work, that she steals food from her and we are not treating her well. Reza is almost convinced."

"No . . . no . . . no. I did not say anything!" Reza interrupted.

"The problem is that originally you did not say anything. You should have said something to your wife. Actually, how would you say anything? You are the one who agrees to everything your wife says. Actually, you and your wife are both jealous of me and my wife and my newborn kid. Isn't that right?"

Both Reza and Doctor Sahib were shocked with Mujeeb's tone and the way he was talking.

"In fact, Reza thinks that he works hard in the shop and we do not do anything for the family. You sit in the shop all day and I am working hard to get our school recognized by the state government, which is also for the family's benefit. And Rizwan works hard in the field to grow crops which is also important." Mujeeb added.

Reza was completely shocked with his elder brother's behavior. Doctor Sahib quickly understood that it was not possible for these brothers to stay together. Because Doctor Sahib was the only child of his father, he had no idea about the brothers' conflict. One thing he could easily understand was that he needed to do something to settle their businesses separately so they could earn their bread and butter without interfering with each other.

Time was flying. Rani struggled a lot at home. She continued working hard despite the fact that she was going to have a baby. She thought that her husband would fight for her rights. She thought that he would understand that when she attended Shakko during her pregnancy and did not let her do any household work that time when she was pregnant Shakko should do the same. However, her husband did not say anything to them. He was not behind her for her rights. Now in the seventh month of her pregnancy he could realize that this was her destiny. She had to do every duty at home. Whatever she got in terms of food to eat, she had to be satisfied with that.

Finally, she decided that if by tolerating all these problems everyone in this home would live in peace then she would do so. After, she did not utter a word of complaint to her husband.

One day she felt a severe pain in her stomach and fainted on the ground. Shakko did not come out of her room. After a few minutes, when Reza entered, he took her into the room and threw a few splashes of water on her face. She came to her senses. She was crying with pain. Shakko came in the room then and said. "This is just a normal pain of pregnancy. Why was she working while I am here to do everything? She actually likes to show other people that she is very hard working. By the way, there is nothing about which to worry. It is a normal pain in this period of her pregnancy." After saying this, Shakko went into her room.

"Did you eat anything?" Reza asked his wife.

"No, I didn't."

"Why?"

"There was nothing left in the kitchen."

"Why?"

"I don't know."

"Hmm . . . Allah will give you a great reward for all the good works you do." he said and suggested that she be patient.

"Only Allah can do justice." she said and wiped her face. Both looked at each other with love.

"If you want to eat something, I can go and get a piece of bread for you from the neighbor." Reza gave her an option.

She did not say anything and went to clean the corridor. While cleaning she fainted. Rizwan informed Reza about it and they took her into the room where she came to her senses and told them that she was having a very bad pain in her stomach.

It did not take a minute for Doctor Sahib to understand that it was not a normal pain. He knew a woman in the next village who was an assistant of a famous gynecologist in the block government hospital. She came and looked at the patient and told doctor Sahib that because she had not eaten anything since morning she was feeling weakness. Because she is a polio patient, chances of becoming a mother for her are very low. Usually a polio patient does not become pregnant. This is nothing less than a miracle that she became pregnant. In this condition, it's good to take her to a hospital and leave her under a good doctor's supervision.

Doctor Sahib understood that it was going to be very costly so it was good to send her to her mother's place where her parents would take care of her.

Reza left home with his wife for his wife's place.

Doctor Sahib was sitting outside the door on a cemented area. He was cleaning his teeth with a brush, which was a piece of a branch from a neem tree. He heard Shakko's voice. She was talking to no one.

"Am I a villain? Why should I hide the food? I have taken care of everybody in the house since I came after my marriage. I think my parents were blinded so they could not see that they were marrying their daughter to a family who is ignorant. They spoiled my life by sending me here to this home." After saying all these things, she began crying. "What was my mistake? Was it that I gave birth to a baby boy who would be called the eldest in the family? These folks are being jealous and trying to accuse me of everything. They are blaming me for all of her health complaints. I was not the one who suggested that Reza marry a handicapped girl. They did it. Now bear with all these," she added. Shakko was not talking to anyone but she was fully aware that Doctor Sahib was sitting outside and listening to her.

Doctor Sahib could not figure out what to do with this situation.

Chapter Ten

On the way to Rani's parent's home, Reza and Rani were sharing their feelings openly without any fear. This was the first time they had been alone.

"See, I love you more than everything but this is my family. My brothers and my father are everything to me so I cannot go against them. It doesn't matter what they do with me. They care for me and they will not think anything except my goodness. I would even sacrifice my life for them. I don't know why you do not understand them and I don't know why they behave like this with you." Reza tried to be apologetic.

"I can tell you what the truth is." Rani began to say. "They love you. They care for you. This is what you think. Maybe it is true. They don't want anyone to love you more than them. This could be one of the reasons that they don't like me. Your father is the only one who cares for me besides you. They should understand that if they love you they should love me too. We are not two. As long as you are with me, I don't have any problem. If they love you that is fine with me but I am afraid that maybe one day they will take you from me. Nothing would be worse than that for me." Rani expressed her views.

Suddenly, Rani felt some pain when the horse-cart jerked. Reza stopped the horse cart and went into a house nearby the road to get some water for her to drink. The road was actually a dam of a canal. Reza got some water for her, made her drink, and helped her to get out of the horse-cart. He took her to one stranger's home and lay her down on a cot, which had been outside of the house. The owner of the house helped them a lot. His daughter made two cups of hot tea for them. They continued their talk.

"What do you think about our baby? Like whom it would look." Rani asked Reza curiously.

"I think it will look like you because you are beautiful." Reza replied happily.

"But I want him to become like you: a perfect religious man, truthful, and a little handsome too." said Rani while rubbing her stomach.

"O yeah, a little handsome." He said and they both laughed. Then they went back to the horse-cart and resumed their journey.

Reza was smiling. He had never seen his wife so happy in the home. For the first time he realized she loved him a lot. She never expressed her feelings though.

"I know what you are thinking." She drew him out of deep thought by patting his shoulder.

"Hmm . . . tell me then what am I thinking."

"You are thinking about your baby's name. Am I right?"

"Yup . . . you are right." he said. Very soon, they could see the border of Rani's village. She was going to her village for the first time after her marriage to Reza. Reza was also exited to meet her family, friends, and relatives.

When the horse-cart reached Hamid's door, many kids came and stood around the horse-cart. Abid, Jawed, and the beautiful Leila came quickly. They saw their elder sister and when Reza tried to pull her out of the cart, Hamid also came to help her out. They thought that she was sick. Rani's mother took her to the bedroom to let her rest. Hamid, his wife, and Reza all sat in the meeting room.

"Is everything alright with you?" Hamid asked.

"Yes, absolutely fine. In fact, because of the medicine shop it was hard for me to leave so I could not come to see you."

"Did you take Rani to doctor yet?"

"No, not yet, because in my house no one was free. My brother Mujeeb had to go to Patna, Rizwan is good for nothing as you all know, and Abba had to stick with his business. So I thought you could take care of her in a better way." Reza said.

"You made the right decision, Son-in-law. We will take her to the doctor tomorrow morning. Let's see what they say and moreover you will be there with us also." Rani's mother said to him.

"Actually, I will not be able to stay here tonight but as soon as I become free, I will come here to see you all." Reza said and apologized.

"Ok, Son-in-law, as you wish." Rani's mother said to him and allowed him to go.

While on the return journey, Reza was busy thinking. "If I have a son then everyone in my family will be very happy but if she has a daughter my family may not accept her and even my wife will be in trouble. Only Allah knows what's going to happen. As per what the lady said, if she dies in this condition before the child's birth . . . . No, this won't happen. Why am I thinking only bad things? I should think about good things instead like she will give me a beautiful baby boy and in my family everyone will be very happy." One after another, ideas and expectations were coming to his mind. He completed his journey from Baqarganj to Kazinagar. When he reached Kazinagar it was evening time. He went into his room and asked for water to make *wazu* (ablution). However for the first time, he realized that he was almost completely dependent on his wife. When he did not get an answer, he took a jug himself and filled it with water. Then after making wazu he went to the masjid.

When he came back he went to the men's sitting room outside. He could not see anybody there. It was pitch dark.

"Who is there? Is it Reza?" Doctor Sahib's voice emerged from the darkness.

"Why are you sitting in the darkness? And where has everybody gone?"

"I know why there is a lot of darkness. In fact, today your wife was not here so there was no one to light the lamp.

"Where is Shakko *bhabhi*? She should have lit the lamp. Not a problem. I am going to get the lamp and light it right now." Reza said and came with a lamp. While he was cleaning the glass of the lamp, Doctor Sahib said to him, "You are the most intelligent son of mine. Always remember, whenever you do anything, that there are many ways, you will find your life but the good way you need to choose. It is very easy to recognize the good way. It looks always uneasy to walk on and less rewarding. Similarly, the wrong way is laden with roses, you can hardly see any thorns on that way, and if you find any, then they will be soft enough to walk on. This is temptation. If you go that way then you will spoil your future here in this world and in the life after death too." Doctor Sahib said to Reza and lay down on a cot nearby, as he was also tired. Reza moved his head in agreement and went inside. After living these many months with his wife he was feeling lonely in his room.

Chapter Eleven

Hamid booked a horse-cart to go to the railway station. The next morning, Hamid and his wife took Rani with them and went to the district town of Betiah to see the most reputed gynecologist of the city, Dr. Neera Chaudhry. The journey in a horse-cart was a little bit difficult for them because of Rani.

When they reached the city they went to the private clinic of the doctor. The clinic was famous as the maternity hospital of Neera Chaudhry. It was the only private hospital in the entire district. When they reached the place, it was very crowded. People were sleeping on the ground. Some of them were sitting on the floor or the wooden bench and some patients and their attendants were standing in the long queue. "Why are they sitting on the ground? The people should have booked a room in the hospital. They may not want to spend money when they can sit and sleep on the ground. It is really mean." Hamid's wife said.

"Let's see what happens with us." Hamid said and told his wife and Rani to stay there until he returned after making inquiry. After a few minutes he came back.

"I need to stand in this queue first to get the patient's name enrolled. Then I need to go there to another window where I need to deposit money. Finally, I need to line up in another queue to meet the doctor." Hamid explained the process.

"Is there any simpler way to meet the doctor?" Rani's mother asked. "Can they not make one window for everything or any easier way to see the doctor?" She added.

"No, this is the procedure to see the doctor. There are other things to do as well. I need to book a room in the hospital to stay tonight because I don't think that after accomplishing all these procedures we will be able to go back home today. And if the doctor suggests that we admit Rani, then we have to admit her here too." Hamid's wife took a bed sheet out of his bag and spread it on the floor outside the clinic in the shadow of a wall. She could not believe that a few minutes ago she was criticizing these people over their situation and now she herself was doing the same. After completing all the formalities and lining up in all three queues for hours, Hamid received only one blank prescription on which the date January 28, 1977, and the enrolment no. 58 was written. It meant that after seeing 57 people, Dr. Neera Chaudhry would see them. It was three o'clock in the evening and they had reached there at eleven o'clock in the morning.

They received word that the doctor was actually not present in the hospital. She was on her way. After lunch, she was supposed to be there at 2:30 pm but she had not yet arrived. It very clearly meant that she would not be able to check Rani that day. Therefore, he needed to book a room as well. After inquiring, they came to know that there was no room available. The room could only be allotted after the doctor's suggestion so they needed to find their own accommodations. Hamid was frustrated after standing in many long queues all day so now he could not find the energy to think of a solution for this accommodation problem.

Hamid's wife thought about her sister who lived nearby whose name was Atia. There were no phone facilities available in those days and they did not know her exact address. At eight pm, the hospital closed so they needed to find accommodation before that time.

Coincidentally, Atia's elder son, who was about Abid's age, was passing by and Rani saw him. He also recognized her and ran to his mother. Atia heard that her elder sister was in trouble so she came quickly and hugged her sister as soon as she saw her. They talked about the situation and decided to go to Atia's home to stay until Rani's delivery.

Early morning the next day, Hamid went to the doctor's clinic as Atia's home was very near to it. The clinic was not yet opened but still, there were quite a few people standing to inquire about the doctor. After inquiring, Hamid learned that, the clinic opened at nine o'clock sharp.

He came back and told Atia to get ready to go to the clinic. When they reached the clinic, there was a queue again but this time, hardly ten to fifteen people were there so he got in line. Doctor Neera Chaudhry got out of her car and the driver ran quickly to close the door. At this time, in the city, only a few renowned people had cars. It was a white Ambassador car. As soon as the doctor arrived everyone in the hospital became suddenly active. The gardeners, the sweepers, the gatekeepers, the assistant of the doctor usually called a compounder and the nurses all became active and got to work. They did not want to be seen sitting when the doctor came.

"Where were you the last seven months?" the doctor scolded someone.

"Madam please, please, madam . . ." the another person was crying.

"Don't waste my time. Get out of here." She scolded again.

"Why did you give her the antibiotic and these painkillers?"

"Doctor, Please . . . Actually she had severe pain so I gave her antibiotics."

"Are you a doctor? Are you? No? Then why did you give her medicine? Why?"

This was all Hamid could hear. After that, the compounder came out and called in a loud voice, "Next!"

Hamid got up and took Rani with him. He was a bit afraid because of the discussion he had heard a minute ago. He went inside. An extraordinary beautiful young lady doctor was sitting there. She seemed to be a very reserved kind of a lady. He was overly impressed. It was hard for him to say anything. She was wearing a sleeveless suit. Having short hair and wearing a sleeveless suit was not yet a trend in Betiah Bihar. Actually, it was not even common in India.

"What happened to you?" The doctor asked.

"Sir . . . sorry . . . madam . . ." Hamid tried to speak but the doctor interrupted him in between. "I am not asking you the question. I am asking the patient." Before Rani could answer or say anything, the doctor continued talking. "It sounds like she is pregnant."

"She is in her eighth month." Hamid spoke and then put his hand over his mouth as he had spoken without permission. He was scared. The doctor looked at him and smiled. "Congratulations! Is she your daughter?"

"Yes Madam." Hamid said.

"You are a very lucky man. Where is her husband?"

"He was busy so he could not come."

"Is he a doctor?"

"No Ma'am."

"Then why is he busy. Anyway, usually a polio-affected girl does not become pregnant. She is lucky."

"You need to go and get this x-ray done and then the blood report is needed by this evening. Only then, I will be in a position to tell you anything. Chances of complications are there but I will be able to conclude only after all the reports. For now, you can buy these medicines. Let me check her pulse." she said and took Rani's hand. "O my God she has got a high fever. You have to admit her."

"Admit her immediately." she called the compounder and told him then gave instruction to send the next patient in.

Hamid came out of the doctor's chamber unable to understand anything the doctor had said so he went to the compounder. The compounder explained everything to him and directed him to go to a specific x-ray center that was almost five kilometers away from there. Though there were several x-ray centers nearby, he used to do this because the x-ray machine owner was his friend. The owner used to give the compounder ten percent of the total income generated by him. No one had the courage to go against the compounder's suggestion. If anyone did so, he did not support him or her at all.

Hamid, according to the doctor's suggestion, admitted Rani into the hospital so the doctor could take care of her around-the-clock.

The next day, Hamid came to the doctor with all the reports. After going through all the hassle of lining up in the queue, Hamid could see the doctor again. The doctor looked at the reports and seemed a little worried.

"This is exactly what I was afraid of. There is no option available to save the child. It is a big complication."

"What happened madam?"

"You cannot understand Hamid Sahib but do one thing, call her husband here. Surgery might be needed."

"Surgery? What?"

"We need to cut her stomach to take the baby out. This is the only way. I can't give you any promise to save the child and for surgery the guardian needs to sign a paper. The paper will say that the guardian has no objection to let the operation be done because the chances of her survival are fifty-fifty. It will be expensive too. However, don't worry. You have time to make a decision. You have the next two days to think about it but within this week the operation should be done."

Hamid listened to the doctor very seriously. He came out of the clinic where Rani's mother and Atia were waiting for him.

"What happened?" Atia asked.

"What did the doctor say?" Rani's mother asked.

He did not reply. He stood there quietly and wanted to hide the situation from them but his eyes gave him away and became red and full of tears. He wiped his face and told them, "Everything is alright. We need to call Reza here somehow. The doctor was asking for him."

Rani's mother could easily understand that something was not right.

Atia said, "I can go to the post office and send a telegram to Reza to let him know that he is needed here." After saying this she left to go to a post office.

When Rani's mother found Hamid alone then she again asked, "What happened? Is everything alright?" Hamid knew that he could not hide anything from his wife. She easily caught his lies.

"He broke down crying and told her in a broken voice that the baby could not be saved and that his daughter could only be saved by surgery.

Surgery was not common in the case of maternity in those days. Most of the deliveries used to happen at home under the supervision of the elderly women of the villages. Hardly two percent of deliveries would happen in the hospital. This was why, as soon as the friends and relatives of Hamid heard about it, they reacted as she was certainly going to die. Most of them had never heard about surgery in their lifetime. The environment of Atia's home turned into mourning.

"There is no chance to save the baby." Rani's mother said and began crying.

"It is not a problem if the baby cannot be saved but Allah, please save my daughter." Hamid became sad and could not stop his tears. Rani's mother, Hamid, Atia and most everyone else were almost crying but at the same time they were trying to hide their feelings from Rani. Rani was not aware of the truth.

Rani was a little bit afraid because of the surgery but happy at the same time. She was happy to think of having a baby. "What will the baby look like? Who will he be like, his father Reza, or like me? If it is a boy then it would be for him to look like his father but if it is a girl then she should be like me." Rani was thinking about her future baby.

"Amma, Reza did not come yet?" Rani said to her mother.

"He must be busy." her mother told her brushing her hair with her fingers.

"Amma, we must buy some baby dresses and toys because after the birth, that will be the immediate need." Rani said with emotion.

"Hmm . . . sure." Her mother wanted to hide her tears so she put a part of her sari over her face but she could not hide her broken voice.

"Are you crying, Amma?" Rani asked.

"Because I am very excited you are going to be a mother for the first time and I will become a grandma. I could not stop my tears." She said and quickly left the room. She stood in a corner, faced a wall, and cried. Atia heard her crying, came there, and she comforted her. She said, "Allah is great. He does justice with everybody. He will not be unjust to you. Brother Hamid had gone to meet the doctor again. Let's see, he may come with a solution. Allah controls everything. Please come and pray for her. Who knows maybe some miracle happen and Allah will save your child and her baby both! Everything is possible with God."

Reza received the telegram. He closed his shop and went home. He was ready to go to Betiah. Mujeeb saw him coming home. He went to his room and talked to his wife about it. Shakko knew that if Reza went to Betiah then he would take some money with him and if the surgery happened then Reza would pay a big amount for it that would the expense of the whole family. She would convince him somehow by hook or by crook to stop Reza from going to Betiah. When Mujeeb came out of his room he saw Reza talking to Doctor Sahib. He was afraid that Reza might be able to convince Doctor Sahib who then might give him permission so he moved forward faster and reached them quicker.

"What's the matter?" he asked.

"He has received a telegram saying that Rani needs surgery and that her life is in danger so he wants to go to Betiah." Doctor Sahib said. "I think he must go there because his wife and his baby's life are in danger. There is one problem; I don't want him to go there without money. She is his liability so he should pay the bills for her." Doctor Sahib further added.

"I think for the approval of the school, I need to go to Patna urgently because today is the final meeting for government approval in the undertaking of the school. After the approval, all three of us brothers will become teachers in the same school and all of us will be called government employees. Therefore, I think I have to go to Patna and Reza should stay here in the shop for the next two days. Then he will be able to go anywhere he wants." Mujeeb suggested.

"No. absolutely not. This is priority. Nothing is more important than Rani's and her baby's life at this time." Doctor Sahib discarded his suggestion completely. Mujeeb found himself losing the battle.

Doctor Sahib went to his room to bring some money for Reza. Mujeeb grabbed this opportunity, came closer to Reza, and tried to convince him not to take the money. "Do you know how much money surgery takes? It's a lot of money. Think of all that you will spend if you go to Betiah. If you don't go then her father and mother are with her. They are not going to leave her on this occasion. If I do not go to Patna today then think about how much of a loss it could be? If the school becomes a government approved school then we will all be teachers. We will get salaries every month. If you don't go you are not going to lose anything anyway. Her parents will do everything possible to save her life. If you don't go then we will save a lot of money. Now the decision is in your hands." Mujeeb tried to convince him. Doctor Sahib came from his room with the money. When Doctor Sahib came Mujeeb left but he had done his job by then. Reza wanted some more time to think about going.

In the hospital, Rani and all her relatives had their fingers crossed.

A nurse came with a file. "Who is the guardian of Rani?" She called aloud.

"I am." Hamid spoke out from the crowd.

"No, I mean where is her husband?" the nurse asked.

"He is busy with his job but it is not a problem. I am here as her guardian. I am her father. You can tell me what to do." Hamid explained.

"What? Her husband is busy? His wife and his first baby are fighting for life in the hospital and he is busy in his job? Wow!" She commented sarcastically. "Is he planning to leave her because she is handicapped and he might know that she and her baby are in danger? Busy in job hnh . . . ." She came with the file to Hamid and told him to sign a couple of places. He signed and then the nurse took Rani to the operation theatre. Atia, her sons, Rani's mother, and a few of Hamid's neighbors were there. The doctor called Hamid and patted him on his back. "I will try my best to save her and her baby both. The rest depends on God. Hamid couldn't say anything.

He remained standing and put both hands together as if she was a straw for a drowning man.

Outside the hospital, people were standing and the operation had begun. This was the first time for Hamid and his family to have heard of surgery and it was for their daughter. Rani's mother fainted. The people in the hospital gathered around her and one of them threw some water on her face so that came to her senses. Everyone was praying for Rani's life there in the hospital.

After half an hour, a nurse came out, got some medical equipment and ran back into the operation theatre. Before she entered, Atia asked her about the situation.

"The situation is very critical but we are trying hard." she said and went in. Hamid and his wife were praying for her life. After one hour they heard a baby cry. The doctor came out.

"Congratulations, Mr. Hamid! You are a grandfather. Your daughter's situation is very critical. Her blood pressure is very low." She went back after saying these things.

They couldn't celebrate the child's birth until they heard the news that Rani was out of danger. Hamid and his wife took a deep breath of relief. However, before they could celebrate, a nurse came gasping. She informed the compounder that the baby was not crying and the doctor was still busy with the patient in the operation theatre. The head nurse, who was an elderly woman, came and suggested that they inform the doctor about it anyways. The doctor took this matter very seriously, came out, and checked up on the child. She said, "The baby needs oxygen immediately! There was no facility to provide oxygen in the city or nearby cities. The doctor did not want to take the risk of sending the child to the other city or the bigger cities so she decided to keep the baby under her supervision. She informed Hamid that the baby was in danger. If he survives for the next twenty-four hours then only will he be saved. Those twenty-four hours were passing like twenty-four years for them.

Reza was busy in his routine life. Going to the shop at six-o-clock in the morning and coming back at nine in the evening. Inside, he was very much concerned about his wife. He was not aware of whether his baby had been born yet or not. He did know how difficult the situation was there without him for Rani and her parents. Doctor Sahib encouraged him many times to go to the hospital to find out about the situation but Reza was quite relaxed because he was fully convinced that without him, there wouldn't be any problem for Rani because her parents were there.

The next morning, when everyone was afraid of the newborn baby's survival in the hospital, Doctor Sahib called Reza and forced him to go to Betiah to find out what happened there. Reza got ready to go to Betiah.

There were a few lawyers in the nearby villages that used to go to Betiah court every day. Atia sent a message to Mujeeb with one of them that Reza had a cute baby boy. About the kind of situation that was happening in Betiah, she could not find the room to send any further detail.

Mujeeb gave this news to the whole family. Once Reza heard that he had a baby boy he blushed and was thrilled with excitement. It was hard for him to believe that he had become a father. He wanted to share this happy moment with someone close. This was the first time that Reza missed Rani a lot.

In the hospital, Rani's mother stayed up all night with the baby in her lap. When she would get tired then

Atia would replace her. Inside, both the sisters were pronouncing God's name.

In the morning, the doctor came to her for the routine check-up of the baby. She did some diagnosis and told Hamid, his wife, and Atia, "I have one good piece of new and one bad piece of news for you. The good news is that the baby is out of danger now and the bad news is that Rani cannot become a mother again. It means that this will be her only child. Moreover, one more thing, you need to protect this baby from hard summers and hard winters for all of his life. Whenever the temperature is very hot or very cold it will be dangerous for the baby's health. All of his life he needs to be taken care of in summer and winter seasons." Dr. Neera Chaudhry said everything in one go without caring about the reaction of the attendants.

"Whatever Allah does is good for us." Atia said and tried to comfort Rani's mother. "You should be thankful to God that you daughter and grandson are alive and healthy." Atia added.

One of the nurses came and asked Hamid to come with her into the office. Hamid went with her. She opened a file before him and asked him to sign a couple of documents.

"What are these papers for?" Hamid asked.

"This is a discharge file. It means that now you are free to take the patient home with you." The nurse informed him.

Hamid was very excited about going home and sharing this news with everybody in the village and their relatives.

Chapter Twelve

Mujeeb came home as happy as if he had won a big battle. He sat on the verandah as a wrestler comes home after winning a tough game. Reza was curious to know what happened with his elder brother. Mujeeb looked dazzled.

"We have the approval from the government to run the minority school." He said gladly.

"Wow! That is big news. It means we all have government jobs. It means we will all become teachers. Wow, nothing can be better than this. No greater news is possible than this." Reza almost shouted with happiness. His excitement turned to the extreme. He wanted to share this happiness with someone very close to him so he called Rizwan and told him, "We have gotten approval for our school. We will all be teachers." All three brothers celebrated this happy moment together.

Reza was filled with joy because he recently became a father and then now there was this other good news.

He was flooded with happiness. He wanted to share everything first with his wife. This had become a part of his habit since he got married so this time also he wanted to talk to his wife. He could not have talked to her until he met her because there was no phone facility in the area so far. Nevertheless, he found a way to talk to his wife. He rode his bicycle and reached his wife's place within an hour.

Abid, who had already said good-bye to education, was nowadays busy with his father in farming. He would go everyday to the field with his father to support him. He saw Reza coming and ran to his home to give the news to his mother before reaching Reza but some other child ran faster than he ran and had already given this good news to Rani. Rani was blushing with joy.

Her father and mother had doubts somewhere in the back of their minds that because their daughter was a handicapped girl, Reza might leave her. The doubt took place because no one from Reza's family even asked about Rani during her pregnancy. For this reason, Hamid and his wife were both very excited to see Reza and at the same time they wanted to show their annoyance.

As soon as Rani saw Reza entering through the veranda, she put her child in the cot and put her right hand or her knee to get up. She used to stand up and walk with the help of someone but she never used a stick because she could always find someone around her who could help her since her childhood. Rani was hoping that Reza would be very excited to see his child and she was not wrong. After entering the home he first took his son in his lap and started kissing him.

Hamid was not available because he went to his lawyer's house to plan for forming a new case so he could trap Rashid in order to send him to jail for his revenge. Reza had a box of sweets in his hand. This was surprising because he did not have this habit of going to his relatives with sweets, as was custom. Rani already guessed that must be something special. Reza waited for a suitable time to share his happiness with Rani. Rani's mother went to the kitchen to arrange some food and water for him. This was a good time for Reza to talk to Rani about the school's approval. When Rani heard this news she smiled and she was very happy to see her husband successful after a long battle with poverty.

Reza wanted to take Rani with him but he could not do that the same day because he had to wait for Hamid so he decided to stay there that night. All day, Reza was busy with his son and talking to Rani. He talked to her a lot about his plans, his son's future, and a lot more. They were both very happy with their only son. Hamid came late at night. At the door when he saw a bicycle, he wondered who the guest was. He had no idea. When he stepped into the house and heard the voice of Reza he felt pleased.

Rani told him later on that Reza came to take her with him. Hamid happily gave them permission to go.

Rani's younger brother Jawed was going to school for his studies. Actually, Hamid wanted him to be sent to the Madrasa hostel but Abid, who had had a bitter experience, did not agree with his father's decision, and insisted that his father let him go to regular school. The school was almost a kilometer away from his home. So on that day Rani prepared him for school. When he was going to school he was a little bit sad because he knew that when he came back, his loving elder sister would not be there at home to welcome him. Rani also could not stop her tears. She gave him a lunch box and stealthily put two extra sweets in it without her mother and father's knowledge. Leila was too young to understand everything. Abid went to hire a horse-cart for them to go. Hamid's wife gave a bath to the baby herself and then she loved him and kissed him.

The next morning, the horse-cart came and Reza and Rani left from there to their home with the baby.

When Reza had left home everybody was happy but when they returned, the environment was completely different. Rizwan was very sad sitting on the outside Verandah. Shakko was in the kitchen and she was not very happy. Doctor Sahib was almost weeping. When they got out of the horse-cart no one was excited. Some villagers were abusing Mujeeb and calling him a 'betrayer.' Reza got down and took his luggage, which was actually gifts from his wife's place, and consisted of two big bags of 30 kilos wheat and rice and two big bags of corn and other grain. Shakko looked at the bags with some surprise because these kinds of gifts had not ever come from her place. Mujeeb came forward and took the baby, kissed him, and loved him. As he saw him for the first time he was very happy. His face did not look very sharp. "Something must have happened." Reza thought.

After putting all the heavy bags in the room, Reza went to Doctor Sahib to find out why everyone at home was sad. Doctor Sahib told Reza that on the list of approved teachers at the school there were only six names instead of twelve. "Is there anyone from our family missing from the list?" Reza asked.

"The problem is not that. The real problem is that Reza already knew about it and he did not tell us. Moreover, he intentionally gave his wife's name in place of Rizwan's. So now, Rizwan will be jobless and Mujeeb and his wife will have a job. There is also one more problem: Mujeeb did not give approval to the three people of this village who worked without any wages." Doctor Sahib told them the whole story.

"How could Mujeeb have done this? It is up to the government who to give approval for appointment and who not to give it to." Reza tried to defend his brother.

"The actual problem was that Mujeeb had done everything because of money because he had already demanded ten thousand rupees from each of the two previous teachers in order to give them appointments. They could not arrange money in the one day that Mujeeb had given them. Now, Mujeeb was going to appoint all of the other six people by taking bribes from them. What my son is doing is disgusting I never taught him to be dishonest and corrupt." Doctor Sahib was very angry and sad.

Reza came out with heavy steps. He went to Rizwan and tried to comfort him.

"Not a problem. I don't have any extra talent. Not a problem. I am not very educated but I can do a lot of things like I can take other people's land and plow it and this is how I can live my life." Rizwan was very disheartened. He wiped his face with a towel and continued talking. "But you got a job. You are a government employee now. I am proud of you. I am going to buy some sweets for you. Believe me; I am very happy for you." The situation was very emotional so Reza left and went to his room. It was lunchtime in half an hour. As usual, Reza came out of his room, washed his hands, and sat on the verandah where all three brothers used to sit and have lunch. He kept sitting there but none of his family members came for lunch. Finally, he went back to his room and asked Rani to bring food. Rani went to the kitchen and was surprised to see that there was no food left in the kitchen. She asked Shakko about the food. "I am not your maid, ok. If you want to eat lunch go and cook." Shakko replied and went into her room. While going into the room she was saying something to herself. "I have a government job and nobody is happy in this family. I worked like a maid for years for this family and still they expect me to be a maid." Rani only heard that much. The rest was spoken very softly in her room. She skipped lunch and did not eat anything but at the dinnertime the situation was the same. This time Rani decided to cook but as soon as she started the process Shakko appeared and began saying, "She wants to take over the kitchen and get me out of all the responsibilities." As soon as Rani heard Shakko's voice, she became speechless and went back to her room.

She could sleep for many nights without dinner but she did not want to let her child sleep without food so she decided to tell Reza to buy some milk separately for her baby. Now Rani understood how difficult it would have been for her mother to survive in the joint family and how difficult it would have been for her to raise children in a joint family. Reza agreed to buy separate milk. Rani used to work at home all day and when she found food left in the kitchen she would eat it. She passed many years this way.

One day she fell very sick. Reza took her to a local doctor who suggested that Reza take her to a district town because it might be a different cause of fever and cough. As per the doctor's suggestion, Reza took her to the district town where the doctor asked for an x-ray. Ultrasound was not available there. It was the evening time so the pathologist told them that the report would be ready by the next day. Rani was very sick. She had a fever and she was coughing badly. Reza bought some fruit for her because nothing else was tasty for her those days. They stayed all night in the hospital. They did not have enough money to rent a room in the hospital, as it was very expensive for them. They spread a bed sheet, which they had carried with them, in the corridor of the hospital. A doctor saw Rani coughing badly and sleeping on the floor. He came to them and suggested they get a room. It did not matter that they were unable to pay they could still avail themselves of a room. He called Reza with him and showed him the room. It was a very good room and well furnished. Reza was very happy. He went to Rani and shared this good news with her. Rani tried to tell him something but she was coughing so badly she could not speak. Reza gave her water and helped her into the room. She got relaxed and said, "The doctor gave money to the watchman for us to stay. How can a doctor be so good?"

Reza and Rani passed the night in the room of the hospital. The next morning, the doctor came and greeted them, "Good morning. How are you feeling now? I have received your report Rani." "Please tell me what is in it sir. Is everything fine and normal?" asked Reza with curiosity.

"I haven't seen the report yet. Why don't you come with me, I will have a look, and then we will talk about it there." The doctor said.

It was quite unusual for Reza that a doctor wanted to talk to him. Reza went with him. The doctor opened an envelope and took out the report. The doctor became serious while reading the report. "Is there some problem doctor Sahib? "Yes, there is. She has tuberculosis." It had no meaning for Reza because he had not heard this word before so he stayed puzzled. "Tuberculosis was an incurable disease until a few years ago. Scientists recently discovered the medicine for it. Now it is curable but for that you need to take certain pills everyday for the next nine months." The doctor was very serious so Reza was a little bit scared. He did not understand what the doctor was explaining.

"Now listen very carefully to what I am going to tell you." The doctor added further. "The medicine for tuberculosis is very expensive in the market but the government is giving some subsidy on these medicines so it's better and cost effective to buy medicines from the government hospitals. The second thing, the course of medicine is for nine months but she needs to take the pills everyday and if she skips one day then the nine-month will be counted from that day once again.

The third thing is you need to take care of her a lot because it is a very dangerous disease. You need to take care of her food. Whatever she likes, buy it for her, but make sure that she always eats. Think that of her food as a part of her medicine. Take it very seriously and remember that many people have died in the past because of this disease. It used to be considered an epidemic.

"You are lucky that a few years ago the treatment for it was invented." The doctor was explaining everything to him as if he were a kid. Reza came from the doctor's chamber with heavy steps. He told everything to Rani. Rani was in deep thought after listening to Reza. She had only one fear that if she died what would happen to her kid. Who would take care of him?

Reza was fully aware of the fact that under the supervision of Shakko it was not possible to take care of Rani's health in his joint family. Therefore, he decided to send Rani to her parents so they could take better care of her there.

Instead of going back home, they went to Hamid's home. Reza patiently told them the whole story and about why he did not want to take her home. He explained everything. Hamid was convinced.

Chapter Thirteen

"**I** knew that she was not a healthy girl. It was a big mistake to choose her for marriage. It wasn't a right choice. Now see the result, she is a TB patient. After a few months she will die and then what will happen?" Shakko, in her usual tone, was saying very loudly.

"I think that instead of wasting much money and time, we should arrange a second marriage for Reza," Rizwan commented.

Doctor Sahib kept listening to everyone but did not comment. He called Mujeeb and asked him to talk to Reza about the whole situation and about what he was thinking.

Reza was a little bit sad.

"I had never ever thought about leaving her and remarrying. It is totally stupid. She is my wife and I have a son with her. I don't want to destroy my family." This was the reaction of Reza when Mujeeb suggested that he remarry.

"What will you do then?" asked, Rizwan. "Will you waste a lot of money on her treatment and wait for her to die and when she will die then will you finally remarry. I don't think it is wise," he added.

"It is really wise. Actually, it is a disease and anyone can catch it. Think about if it had happened to you or me. Would you have said the same thing? I will spend money on her treatment no matter if my family is with me or not. She is the mother of my son. I can't leave her alone in this condition. I am not going to remarry. She got this disease because this family did not take care of her. Even if I remarry the same thing will happen with my second wife also." Reza said everything he wanted to without fear. Shakko was listening to him while hiding in her room. Now it was hard for her to stay calm so she came out and began yelling at Reza. "What do you think? You think that I am the cause for your wife falling sick! If you are thinking this then it means you are sick too. You also need some treatment. No one could find a better home manager than me." She spoke as much as she could and started crying. Mujeeb came and comforted her.

Now Reza understood why his wife fell sick and why she used to complain about the family. He decided not to live with this joint family but again he thought for a few minutes, went to Rizwan, and told him, "See Rizwan! I don't want to live in this joint family anymore but I don't like to give you trouble. I am aware that you do not have a job and that is because of your loving respectable elder brother and his wife. I am tolerating everything only because of you. I have decided to divide everything including father's property, kitchen and this house. What is your opinion?" Reza asked Rizwan.

Rizwan's face turned red as soon as he heard Reza. "If you have already decided to break the family and the family is going to fall apart and split into pieces then please do not show me this false compassion. I am very much comfortable with my elder brother. You might throw me out but he won't. If he does then I will find a solution on my own. I am mature enough to handle my life. I am not a child so please . . . ." Rizwan was almost shouting. Reza did not hear him and left.

Reza was lying on the bed. He was busy recalling golden memories of his childhood, how his brothers were his biggest support how that time had changed. He was feeling lonely. He could not hide his worry. He touched his face and found that it was wet.

It is true that a father can easily understand his son's feelings. Doctor Sahib came into the room, sat behind his head, brushed his hair with his fingers, and said, "Don't worry! I am always with you my son. This time had to come. I think this is the best time to start your life on your own and stand on your own feet. I am always with your decision. Don't ever think that you are alone. I have some contracts and I am going out of the district for some days. I will be back in a week's time so make sure that you don't do anything wrong before I come back." After this he went off.

Reza felt a little bit energetic because of his father's support. He was always bad about making decisions on his own. After this incident, all three brothers did not talk as they used to. There was kind of a cold war going on. They were all waiting for their father, Doctor Sahib, to come back.

Rani was not feeling well. She would cough very badly and sometimes she would get a fever too. Hamid and his wife took care of her very well. The baby was also there with his grandma. His grandma loved him more than anyone.

Hamid succeeded in trapping Rashid in one of the property disputes. Rashid was about to be arrested. Hamid's long wait was going to come to an end. Abid was also very happy because he went to the field several times and saw the injustice of his own uncle. Jawed had nothing to do with all that, as he was busy with his school friends all day. Jawed was so unaware of everything that he played cricket with Rashid's son all day on the same day when Rashid was busy with his lawyers trying to understand the case and find a way out of the legal property issue.

Hamid's wife was feeling a little bit insecure for her. She had a fear that Reza might leave her because she was handicapped and she had tuberculosis. She tried to share this fear with Rani and Hamid but Hamid did not take it seriously.

Rani told her "I don't care. I have my baby boy so I will wait till he becomes an earning body and after that I won't need anyone to support me."

She was proud of her son. "It will take at least sixteen to seventeen years and it will be a long wait." Her mother told her.

"Time flies very quickly," she added.

Her mother came forward and kissed her forehead and said, "May Allah bless you! I only regret that I was not able to give you a good education. In fact, I could not give any of my children a good education. So always remember to educate your child as much as possible."

Rani took her son into her lap and told him, "I will educate you no matter what it takes. I will do everything to educate you. I would like to see you be a professor so you can serve society. This is my dream. After that, I will get everything I ever wanted in my life, money, name, fame, everything. When people call me your mother when you are a professor, I will be proud of you. And I am sure your father will also be proud of you . . . ." She continued saying this to her mother until she began coughing.

Her mother brought a glass of water for her and said, "The first step of your dream is to take care of your health. All of your dreams are possible only when you are healthy. Try to keep yourself healthy."

The police came to Rashid's house to arrest him. Hamid was very anxious to see him go to jail but someone came in a big car and talked to the police officer and they left without arresting Rashid. This incident was very disappointing for Hamid because he had waited for a long period to see this moment so he felt like he had failed. At the same time, he remembered his lawyer's claim that no one could save him. He would have to bite the dust of jail. Hamid was getting out of control. He felt that if his lawyer came he would kill him. Many people had surrounded Rashid's home and were watching this.

Hamid did not want to see all that so he went into his room. As soon as he entered somebody knocked on his door.

"Who is it?" Hamid almost shouted.

"Police!" He heard the voice and opened the door. There were two policemen and his lawyer standing at the door.

Hamid, hiding his anger, tried to smile and welcomed them inside.

"It was actually a bail-able warrant against Rashid so this time he escaped but this time I am going to frame the kind of case against him in which he will not be able save himself. He will have to be in jail for at least a minimum of a couple of week's time so please do not worry." His lawyer assured him very confidently. Hamid had no choice except to trust him so he smiled and replied, "I am ready to wait until the end of my life but I want to see him behind bars at any cost. I cannot forget that fearful night in the jail. What was my fault? I was not a criminal." Hamid told his lawyer.

Chapter Fourteen

Doctor Sahib got a job in a contract company. He had to go to Samastipur for his job. He went by bus. It was a Bihar Road Transport Corporation Bus. It was very crowded and going at a maximum speed of 40kph. The bus sounded like it was more than thirty years old. The driver's age was above eighty. Some people were smoking inside the bus, which was quite normal on this route. Only one third of the passengers could get a seat and all the other people were standing. Because of the crowded conditions, people stood on each other but no one complained. They knew that it was the matter of only two hours.

Doctor Sahib always wanted to see his children united and together which seemed impossible now. He was bit worried and happy at the same time too because his sons had the government job. Still Rizwan was not settled. He thought that if he would tell this to his boss then maybe he would find a job for Rizwan. The chain of his thought broke with the blowing horn of the bus then he realized that he had reached his destination. He went to his boss and talked about his son's job. His boss gave him a positive response because he was quite impressed with his honesty, integrity and truthfulness. He felt very happy inside for Rizwan. He had to go outside of the city to deliver some goods and then after coming back, as per the plan, he would be paid his salary and then he would go home and come back in a week's time with his son. However, God had a different plan for him. After delivering the goods to his boss's partner in another city he came back.

He was a very connected and social person by nature. Wherever he had lived in his life so far, he had made many friends. Whenever he crossed the streets of Samastipur, he had a habit of greeting every shopkeeper in the street. Because of this, everyone recognized him and paid respect to him.

It was Friday morning when he was coming back after Friday prayer. On the way, as per his habit, he greeted many people. After coming from the Jama Masjid, he was on the way to his house in the town. He bought some *tilkut* on the way and chewed them. When he was walking over the railway flyover, he felt a pain in his chest and fell down on the bridge. He lay unconscious on the bridge until other people who were coming from the mosque saw him, took him, and went to the hospital nearby. People who heard this on the street, rushed to the hospital. After a few minutes a doctor came with a stretcher. Doctor Sahib was lying on it and his face was covered with a white sheet. On his beard some chewed tilkut stuck and was not looking nice. "Before coming here he was already dead," the doctor said. The mob was sad and started whispering to each other about his goodness. Let his sons know about it.

"Who will take this dead body to his home?" someone asked.

"I will." A priest of a temple took the initiative very quickly. It was a little strange that many Muslims were there but no one came forward for this work. A old Muslim man who had a beard and was a practicing Muslim died and a Hindu priest was saying that he would take the dead body home. How was that possible? India is infamous now for its hatred against Muslims but things were not so bad at that time.

"It is actually a result of his good behavior," one young man said. "But this priest doesn't know the correct Muslim culture and tradition to treat the dead body so I'll also go with him." A jeep was hired. Nobody knows who paid for it. The jeep reached the man's house at ten o'clock at night.

Rizwan and Reza were busy fighting. Mujeeb was not available but he received this message that his father was sick so he was on his way. As soon as the jeep reached the village, they blew the horn. Almost half of the villagers rushed out and surrounded the jeep to see the dead body.

The villagers washed the dead body. Mujeeb did not return home until 11pm and came to know that his father was no more. He began crying like a child.

After the special prayer called *Namaz-e-janazah,* people took the body to the graveyard and buried it.

With his burial, a chapter was closed.

A generation ended.

The door of old values was shut.

A few of the old men were trying to recall the good memories related to him. "He did not ever cheat at games when he was a child." one old man said sitting and leaning to the wall. "May Allah bless him." the other old man said. "We were very sad when he travelled to Bangladesh but still we had this hope that someday he would come back but now . . ." He wiped his face, took his stick, and left for home.

"Let's see how his children carry his succession." the people there started whispering.

The next day, Reza left for his wife's scheduled check-up. The doctor told them that Rani had showed a big improvement and that maybe after one month she wouldn't even need to come back to the hospital. When Reza heard that he became very happy. He was happy not only because she had gotten well but also because he would not need to travel anymore. He went to his wife's place once again to share this good news with Rani's parents.

They were also celebrating because by this time Hamid had succeeded in achieving his long-standing goal of revenge. He and his lawyer succeeded in framing Rashid and Rashid had been sent to jail. When Reza, Rani, and their son went to see Hamid, he was not available because he went to meet Rashid in jail. Rashid was sitting behind the bars. He sat as a player sits when he is defeated badly and unexpectedly in a game. Hamid waved his hand and asked, "How are you brother?" Rashid had nothing to say except a few bad words.

"Hamid laughed and told him, "Brother you are the one who started the game and I finished it. But don't worry brother, you will act out soon and after that, we will live in peace." Hamid offered to finish this rivalry forever.

"Peace? What do you mean by this? You have sent me to jail. You come to see me here and now you are telling me to live in peace? Do you really think that I will let you live in peace? If you think so, then it means either you are a fool or you think that I am a fool. You came here to make fun of me. Right? Remember, when I get out of jail, I will not be as nice as I used to be with you. I will make your life hell." Rashid was very angry. Hamid wanted him to get angry. The way Rashid spoke to him gave an immense pleasure to Hamid.

Rashid's daughter was getting married. The date of the marriage was fifteen days later. Rashid wanted to get out of jail as soon as possible.

Rani was waiting to see her father. Hamid was coming towards his house. When he crossed the graveyard he was not afraid but still he started saying a few words of the Quran to himself. "This was the same road I came after being released from the jail. I had not made any mistake or broken any law so why did he frame me? Why did he send me to jail? Now he himself is reaping what he planted."

On the way, he saw a tree. One of the branches was very low. He went to it, sat down on the branch, and started shaking it. He did not know why he was doing so. Suddenly tears emerged from his eyes. This was the same branch, on which all three brothers used to play. At that time, Rashid loved his younger brother more than anyone did. He stood up from the branch, went behind the tree, and started looking for something near the root of the tree. "This was the same place where I hid the stick. How's it possible that I cannot find it. The stick is not here," he mumbled.

When Father Haji Sahib was looking for Rashid to beat him because he ran away from his studies, at that time Hamid hid his stick under this tree to save Rashid from his father. Hamid still remembered that his father became very worried about that stick. He could not find in and in the end he went home. Three days after that incident, Rashid and Hamid were again playing under this tree where Hamid disclosed this secret to his brother Rashid and within a month, their father died.

Hamid was busy thinking about his childhood when someone called him. He cleaned his glasses and tried to see. It was his lawyer.

"What are you doing here?"

"Nothing."

"What a coincidence. Before going to jail, your brother was also sitting here. I was shocked when I saw him smiling. He was holding a very dirty stick. He kept looking at it and smiling," the lawyer said to Hamid. "I asked him the same question, "What are you doing?" He answered the same as you answered. "Nothing." You both are very similar in behavior," the lawyer added.

Hamid did not comment. The lawyer helped Hamid reach home because it was dark.

Hamid's wife was feeling very happy because she had heard the good news about Rani and because her husband succeeded in his mission so he would not burn her with plans and schemes anymore.

Rashid was worried about his daughter's marriage. He began thinking about getting revenge over this jail incident. He met his lawyer, told him to think about the revenge, and to prepare false cases against Hamid. This time, he wanted to frame Abid and Jawed too because it would be a greater pain for Hamid.

Hamid finally reached home where, another piece of good news was waiting for him.

Chapter Fifteen

Living in a joint family for ten years and living separately for many years was full of thorns for Rani. The time passed as it always passes; it doesn't matter whether it leaves good memories for you or it horrifies you when you look back.

A very handsome boy in funky dress used to move around the village. He was in his twenties and his mother Rani was in her forties. Rani had a big dream for her son. She wanted to send him to a university, as she wanted to see him be a professor someday. There were two reasons. One was because it is a respected profession and the other reason was that she wanted him to support her in the fight against poverty. She had tolerated all the pain in her life waiting for good days. Now, she could see the chances for her dream to come true soon. Her son graduated with his bachelor's degree in Urdu literature and now his father Reza was trying hard to gather money to pay the fees for his further education.

Rani's health was not very good because of the long illness. She looked very weak. Reza also looked older than his age because he had faced many ups and downs in his life. Nowadays he did not think about his second marriage anymore as he used to think about it a few years ago whenever his wife fell sick or went to her place for a few weeks.

Anas went to the college nearest his house, which was around three kilometers away. He used to walk there. However, the University was around ninety kilometers away from his house so Anas would have to live away from his home. After admission he would have to go to the district town and rent out a room to live there so of course, the budget would be higher than before. Reza talked to his wife many times trying to convince her that the cost of higher education was not within their budget. They could not afford it so she should leave the idea of Anas getting a higher education and send him to Mumbai or Delhi instead to earn some money would be a great support to them. However, Rani was not ready to compromise her son's education. She wanted her son to be educated at any cost.

Reza decided to earn some extra money besides his job for his son's education but he could not find a way. Rani used to raise chickens as her hobby so she advised Reza to turn this hobby into a profession. He agreed and very soon they ended up opening a nice average poultry farm. They started it in Anas' room as they were planning to send Anas to the district town to study.

Anas went to the University. This was the first time for him to go to a big city so he was amazed. He looked at all of the big buildings of the University very curiously. For the first time, he saw girls and boys holding each other's hands and walking closely. He went there to get admission in the master course of Urdu literature.

After passing through many beautiful departments of study, he reached the filthiest and ugliest looking series of departments of languages and literature while the science departments were very nice and well maintained. He entered into the department of Urdu where some animal poop and a few mice welcomed him. He decided not to take admission and go back to his home but when he entered inside he changed his mind.

"Did you come to take admission here?" a sweet voice of a young girl attracted him.

"Yes," he said and he was too overwhelmed to utter a word because there were four or five extraordinarily beautiful girls standing there. The girls understood that he was not feeling comfortable because he was busy looking at them from head to toe. One of the girls came forward and tried to make him comfortable.

"Did you come here for admission or have you taken admission already?"

"This is my first day here and I came only to inquire."

"What do you want to inquire about? Maybe I can help you."

"Actually, I would like to find information about the admission procedure."

"I can help you with that." She explained the admission procedure and the other three girls were helping her to give the information about how to gain admission. A girl in a pink suit standing behind them did not say anything. She was only smiling. He wanted to see her. He tried to see her. The other girls understood that he wanted to talk to her so they moved a little bit. She was very thin and she had a very small face. He liked her smile a lot and wanted to talk to her.

"Can you please help me to fill out the form?" he asked.

"We are here to help you fill out the form. Why do you want her help?" the other girl asked him with naughtiness and along with the other girls laughed out-loud. Anas also laughed and said, "No . . . nothing special . . . yes anyone of you can help me of course . . ."

"By the way, my name is Hena." she said and offered her hand to shake. He shook her hand and didn't say anything. He continued to stare at her. He could not say anything until she asked his name.

"O . . . . o . . . I am sorry . . . my name is Anas . . . I am kind of like a little lost person . . . Sorry about that."

"No need to say sorry . . . Just like most of the Urdu poets . . . all thinkers look lost. Do you write poetry?"

"No . . . not at all. But I write short stories."

"Ok good. Who is your favorite storywriter in Urdu? I am sure you like Manto."

"No."

"Then Bedi?"

"No."

"Then I am sure you like Krishn Chandra. Am I right?"

"No."

"Oops."

"My favorite writer is Qurratulain Hyder."

"But she is not lost. Right?"

"Right, but . . . stream of consciousness!"

"I agree."

"You are very pretty."

"I agree. And you are very interesting."

"I agree."

"See you again later."

"Or maybe in the class."

The first experience of meeting Hena was memorable for Anas. It was the first time he had had much of a conversation with any girl. He filled out his admission form and went to the University administrative building to complete further admission formalities.

He used not to care about his clothes but unusually he wore formal dress today and stood against a mirror, which was not his habit. He was humming too. He took his bag and left his home for the University.

It was the first day's class of the session. The class was full. The only girls sat on the first row of the bench on the left side. On the right side row he found a seat so he sat. The teacher, Professor Qadri, entered and asked questions about the progressive movement.

"How many of you know about the progressive movement?" the professor asked. Everyone raised their hands thinking that the professor would ask one of them to tell about it.

"Good." the teacher said and asked everyone to write a page about the progressive movement that nobody wanted.

"Maybe the progressive movement means the poets and writers who had progressed a lot or maybe it is about something else?" Anas was puzzled, as he had no idea that what the progressive movement was. "None of the Urdu writers made progress. What should I write? None of them received recognition when they were alive." He had not started to write in his journal when he saw Hena turning her page over and the other students as well. It meant they had written the answer. The teacher asked for everyone's journals. Hena handed her journal over to the teacher first and then everyone else did too. In the end, Anas also gave his journal to the professor, as he could not find any option to avoid doing so.

The professor called the name of the person he thought had written the best answer.

"Who is Shariq?" the teacher called. One fat boy stood up from the backbench. Everyone looked back to see him as the teacher praised his writing a lot. After that, the second name he called was "Hena." He gave his reaction to her writing in a few words and then he carried forward. Anas thought that after four or five journals the teacher would leave but he checked each paper. When he picked up the journal written by Anas, the teacher made his eyes bigger and looked closely at each sentences. Anas was worried that if the professor gave a negative comment then it would be a big insult.

"Who is Anas?"

Anas stood up.

"What have you written? What is this? Could you please read it to the class so your classmates can find out what you mean? Sorry, but I could not understand what you wanted to say." Professor Qadri almost shouted.

Anas remained standing but he could not utter a word. After that, Prof. Qadri read a few lines from the journal a little loudly and the whole class laughed at him. Hena also smiled.

This was so embarrassing for him that after the class, he could not say even hello to anyone. He just left the class and decided not to come again. When he was going out, he saw Hena and found her smiling. Anas thought that she was making fun of him. He did not try to look at her again and he left the building. He returned to his hostel. At first he thought to quit but later on he realized that this was not something about which his mother dreamed. It was very difficult to face. In the hostel was his room partner named Zafar. He was already a final year student of Urdu. He also advised Anas not to quit, as he would help him in learning the Urdu language. He stayed in the city and studied Urdu with him. Zafar used to get books from the library for him and he would read. After that they would discuss the readings. After one month, he again decided to go to the University.

This time, the situation was completely different. Shariq and Hena became friends. They treated Anas as if he was someone who did not know anything. Shariq was more interested in Hena than study. It was only the second day in one month that Anas had gone to the University. It was again for a class of Prof. Qadri's. On this day, he gave a few couplets of Mirza Ghalib to the students to explain. In the last month, he had taught the students how to brief couplets and this day was the assessment day. Surprisingly, he found that Anas's explanations were the best ones among all the students. This was the day when Anas found himself equal to the other students. Other students also considered him a good student. Very soon, all of the classmates became very good friends including Hena, Shariq and Saba.

One day after the class, all of the friends decided to walk until they crossed the main gate. They were walking and talking about Urdu literature. They all were discussing about who was the greatest poet of Urdu literature.

"I think Mir was the greatest poet of Urdu." Saba set the stereotype.

"No, in fact, Ghalib was the best poet." Shariq challenged and looked at Anas to find support for his opinion.

"What thought can you find in Mir's poetry? None. It was all his own life experience.

Look at Ghalib's poetry. He had vision." Shariq added further.

"But Poetry is not made for vision and philosophy. Poetry is, in fact, the voice from the heart. Poetry should be romantic. Good poetry touches everyone's heart. It should be all about what you feel." Hena supported Saba's stereotype.

"You are right. Poetry is a fragile thing. It cannot carry vision and philosophy. The content of poetry should be just what you feel." Anas took this opportunity to stand with Hena.

Hena smiled and felt very happy because she got more support for her standpoint.

All of them were talking when Prof. Qadri passed by. He heard them talking and smiled.

Very soon, the clouds turned black and the wind started blowing. It seemed like it would rain.

"Wow, the weather is becoming very romantic." said Hena, and looked up to the sky.

"You are right. Don't you think that we should spend some good time all together?" asked Shariq.

"Ok let's go to a nearby restaurant," suggested Anas.

"That's the best idea. I was also thinking the same." Hena added. Anas blushed.

"I have written a poem and I will sing some lines of it. In this romantic weather, nothing could be better than that," said Sharique. They all decided to go to a restaurant named "Krishna Restaurant" in front of the gate but before they could reach there, it started raining. Everyone's clothes, including Hena's, became wet. They somehow reached the restaurant. It was completely empty so they settled down. Hena sat close to Anas. Shariq did not feel good to see Hena sitting next to Anas. Shariq opened up his notebook.

"Please do not spoil this extraordinary moment with your philosophical poetry. Sing something romantic," said Saba.

"Not Ghalib type, ok?" Hena teased him.

"Ghalib was also romantic. He was not only visionary and philosophical. Have you not heard *Dil-e-Nadaan tujhe . . . .*"

He started singing a very romantic poem. Hena was impressed and began praising Shariq and his poetry. Anas was getting jealous.

After finishing the poem, they ordered some food. The rain stopped. Before leaving from there, Shariq invited everyone over for his birthday party. The party was on Sunday at his home.

Chapter Sixteen

Rani's hair turned white. Her long sickness and the long wait for good days made her face wrinkled. After separation from the joint family, her life was very peaceful but she always felt lonely especially since Anas had left for the city to study. The city was not far from the village but it usually took two hours by bus.

Anas was unusually extraordinarily happy on that day. He sat beside his mother near the stove. It was not a gas stove. This stove was made of clay and it needed wood or leaves as fuel. Every day she woke up early and cleaned her home. After that, she used to cook breakfast and lunch and then she waited for her husband to come back from the school. This had been her everyday routine since Anas went to the city to study.

"How is your study going?"

"It is going fantastic, Ammi."

"I am in the MA program right now. After finishing it, I will enroll for a PhD and then I will fulfill your dream. I will become a professor."

"This is not only a dream my son. This is a mission you need to accomplish. I could not study. Your maternal uncles could not study because our father was not very aware of the value of education but I want to help you in getting education as much as I can. Tell me one more thing. There will be many other students with you, who also have an aim to become a professor. Tell me about them."

"Yes Ammi. There are many students with me but Shariq is extraordinarily talented. He will become a professor sooner than I will and there is a beautiful girl named Hena. She is also very talented and very beautiful too. On this coming Sunday, is Shariq's birthday. Hena is also coming to the party. I am confused about what to wear for that party." Then Anas stood up and entered his room dancing.

Mother is mother and she understood everything. She understood everything Anas said and those things that Anas did not say.

Technology was growing day by day and had started becoming a part of people's daily life. Electricity was now everywhere. Basic phones were installed in all small markets and post offices by the government. Some rich people also had phones in their homes.

Rani was now happy with her life because her son's life was on track. Her husband was now a government teacher and besides that, because he was a chemist, he started treating people as well. It was illegal to suggest medicine to people without having a medical degree but who cares. People did not care. They only wanted someone who could suggest medicine to them and if it worked, then that person was no less than God to them was.

One day, Rani started coughing. Rani wanted to see the doctor but Reza told her not to worry. All the villagers followed his suggestions and Reza wanted to try his own medicines on her.

"It will be better if we see the doctor." Rani said.

"What will the doctor do? He will prescribe the same medicine I am giving to you and he will prescribe many unnecessary and expensive tests."

"You are educated Reza! I am an uneducated woman. Please do whatever you think is best.

Reza thought for a minute and told her to get ready to go to the doctor. The next morning they went to the doctor. The doctor had some doubts so he suggested some tests.

"I told you that doctors only prescribe expensive tests for commission from the pathologists. I have decided that I will not go with this doctor's advice. I will give you my own medicine. You only have a cough and fever so I know what to do for it. You need some pills for fever and a cough syrup. That's all." said Reza and left for home.

~∞∞∞∞~

Hamid, his wife and Rashid became very old and had retired from their jobs a long time ago. Now their gusto for fighting had also lessened. Hamid could succeed in sending Rashid to jail for two nights. They both no longer wanted to fight. They were sick and tired of fighting. Neither of Hamid's sons could go for higher education as Hamid's wife wanted. When his relatives asked him about their education, then Hamid understood the loss of lack of education. Most of Hamid's relatives were highly educated and were working at respectful designations. Hamid became too old to think about his kid's future. Now he only had one thing to think and that was about his health. Abid had had three daughters and two sons. Abid now understood the value of education so he began giving his full attention to getting his kids educated as far as possible. Because arranging marriages for the girls was not easy nowadays, everybody asked at the time of marriage about the girl's education. In fact, they ask about the girl's father's education as well.

Abid was busy working hard at farming to earn his living, which was very difficult for him. Jawed tried new businesses but they always failed because of his lack of education. He did not have a job but he was waiting for Hamid's death so he would be able to sell some property and would try some more new businesses as well. With all the difficulties, he was also trying to teach his kids too. He had one daughter and one son.

Chapter Seventeen

Hena went home and started planning to go to Shariq's birthday party. Hena understood that Anas might have fallen in love with her but she always thought that Shariq was a good student and he was also interested in her. She had a tough time deciding what to do about this situation.

Finally, on Sunday, all of the students came over to Shariq's home to celebrate his birthday. Hena had put on make-up and she wore nice party wear. She looked very pretty. Shariq wore a *sherwani* on his birthday he also looked very handsome. No one else was in Shariq's home except his mother. His father lived in Saudi Arabia and worked for some travel company. His mother was very beautiful. She was old and had some wrinkles on her face but she was very conscious about her dress. When Reza said hello to her she only smiled and did not talk at all. She was a follower of the old culture and values. When Hena told her hello, she nodded her head with a smile.

Hena knew the old values so she entered her room and sat near her. Shariq's mother took her face in her hands and said, "Very beautiful! Like a moon!"

"Aunt! May I ask you a question?" Hena asked politely. "Hmm."

"What will you do when your heart tells you to do something else and your mind contradicts that? Will you follow your mind or your heart?" Hena asked.

Before she said anything, Shariq entered the room quoting a famous Urdu couplet.

"*Bekhatar kood para atish-e-namrood mein ishq*
Aql hai mahu-e-tamasha-e-lab-e-baam abhi"

(Translation: Love jumped into the *namrood's* fire fearlessly/the brain is yet busy in watching this drama.)

They both smiled. Shariq's mother seemed like she came from a feudal background. Shariq disclosed the story that once his father migrated to Pakistan at the time of partition and left his family behind. Hena was very inspired by and impressed with his mother.

Anas saw and heard everything stealthily. Then they went into the courtyard of the house. Shariq cut the cake and offered some to Hena. Hena took the piece in her hand and fed it to his mother then everybody celebrated his birthday with happiness and joy. Shariq sang a beautiful *Ghazal* (Urdu genre of poetry). After that, everybody clapped. After that, they all went to eat lunch but Hena was not there and no one was looking for her either. Anas became a little worried but he did not want to ask anyone because he did not want anyone to know that he cared for her. He took his plate, began moving around, and found out that she was sitting with Shariq's mother in her room with her lunch.

After some time, the party finished. Hena stood up to go. Shariq's mother wiped her tears and said good-bye to her.

They all left for their homes but on the way, Anas was thinking about how courteous Hena was. His feelings of love for her became deeper. Shariq was very happy because he thought that he had impressed all of his classmates with the party.

When Anas talked to his mother, he told her everything that happened at the party. This time, Rani, the mother of Anas, began asking a few more questions about the girl Hena, and Anas kept giving details about her. Anas was shocked when she asked about his desire to marry her. He could not say anything for a minute but finally he said yes.

After that, Anas forgot about the incident and was busy preparing for exams the same as everyone in the class. Until then, Hena had already decided to choose Anas for life but she was too shy to admit that to Anas. However, she was very frank with her mom so she told to her mom about her feelings.

Just before the exam, a common friend of Reza and Hena's fathers came to Reza and talked about making this proposal formal but Reza refused and told him to postpone until their exam finished.

After finishing the exam, Shariq was a little upset because he realized that Hena had fallen in love with Anas but he never wanted others know that he was upset. However, it is impossible to hide feelings of love and hate. They are like fragrance or smoke. All of the students understood that he was upset. After exams finished, all of the boys became busy finding good universities for higher education to apply for and all the girls stayed at home to wait for their marriages.

Anas chose to go to Delhi University for higher education. He got admission in the M. Phil program. His mother did not want her son to go that far but she could understand the value of education so she allowed him to go. Hena, as other girls, stayed at home and waited for her marriage. While Anas was busy in his studies, his father was planning for his marriage. The date of engagement was fixed.

When Anas came home, he was not aware that he was going to be engaged. He was surprised when he saw that his father came to receive him at the station with a few other relatives. He stood stunned. Very soon, he adjusted himself to this shocking good news. His mother had a key role in getting this engagement done.

Her cough was getting worse and worse.

By this time, Reza had figured out that something was not right with her so there was a need to get her checked by the doctor properly.

Chapter Eighteen

Rashid and Hamid agreed to leave fighting a few years previously but still a cold war was there between both families. One day when all of Rashid's sons were outside of the village to attend a marriage party, Rashid felt little pain in his chest. He went in his room and slept. No one could have guessed that he was sleeping for forever. He died.

Hamid was the one who got this shocking news first. He was the only one who cried for him for many months. After Rashid's death, people came to know how much love and affection was there between both brothers.

It was the end of an era.

After Rashid's funeral, the world saw the unity in this village. People came closer to each other, they respected all elders and loved everybody but this peace could not continue longer. Their sons carried the tradition.

When Rani heard the news of Rashid's death, she could not cook on that day and could not eat for many days.

After Rashid's death, the sons began fighting with each other for property as dogs fight for a bone. Rashid had one daughter too but she had died several years previously. She had two sons. They wanted a share in Rashid's property as well. Someone told them that if a child died when his or her father was alive then there was no right to property for their kids. However, they had planned everything well. They had already talked to a lawyer who knew that this was not the case. In fact, according to the Indian law, they had a right to claim. It was only rumor that they did not have a right. There was a basis for this rumor. According to the Muslim personnel law, if a son or daughter dies when his or her father is alive then his or her children have no right to claim the property. However, Muslim personnel law had no legal approval by the government of India so they could claim. In short they all again began the legal fight and they sold all the property piece by piece. After that they did not have money to fight or to eat.

The similar situation was there with Hamid's family as well. They all started fighting like dogs.

Rani was already sick and Rashid's death made her a little more so. Finally Reza decided to take her to a doctor in the district town. The doctor misdiagnosed and began prescribing the medicine for black fever. Rani was not getting better. Instead, she began coughing more than she used to. Doctors in the district town had the mentality not to prescribe the patient too many tests so they would not lose their patients. Tests were expensive and people there were mostly uneducated so both wanted to avoid tests. However, doctors could guess the problem by the patient's look.

In Rani's case, the guess was not right. At the time of coughing she felt pain in her stomach. After taking pills prescribed by the doctor, she felt very bad and uneasy. She felt severe pain. Reza noticed it but he thought that maybe it was because her body weight was low. A doctor had prescribed these medicines so there was no chance of harm but if the problem continued then he would tell the doctor. After a continuum of complaints from Rani, Reza decided to take her to the doctor but he postponed it until Anas got married.

Hena was very happy because she was going to get married and the person she was getting married to was known to her. Many times she stood in front of the mirror and blushed. She knew that she broke Shariq's heart but she did not feel guilty. She knew that it was not her mistake. Shariq understood it and he did not ever complain.

All of Hena's friends were jealous of her so when they heard that she was getting married and she was getting married to Anas they started gossiping about it and they all decided to boycott the marriage. Although Anas contacted Shariq he could not meet him because after exams he had left the city and moved to his village for a year with his family.

Chapter Nineteen

The first thing that happened in the marriage was that both the parties of the groom's side and the bride's parents sat together and called a religious expert to set a sacred date for marriage which would suit both parties. The *Maulvi* came and looked into a small booklet and suggested a few dates. After one hour brainstorming, they both agreed on the date of February 14. Then the bride's father served laddu to everyone present.

They both began preparation for the marriage ceremony. They went to a cook to find whether he was free on that date or not. There were many famous cooks available in the market but because of Valentine's Day, most of them were not free. Reza called one of his old friends who used to be a cook. After that, Reza went to the printing press shop to order invitation cards. He took his younger brother Rizwan with him. After wasting two to three hours, they chose a card design to order. Finally, after placing the order, they went to a meat shop and other shops to order food items. They had lot to do outside, as they needed to book a car for the groom and then hire someone to decorate it. He arranged everything after a week's hard work.

Many women in the neighborhood used to come to his house. Rani talked to them and she called them to celebrate this happy moment with music. They all sat together in the room and sang marriage songs. Rani wrote a letter to her parents to invite them on this happy occasion. The groom was not allowed to do any work at home. He had to sit and watch everything happening. It was a custom in the village, that the groom, who is getting married, should not cross the borders of the village for seven days prior to the date of marriage. Because Anas was the only child of his parents, it was very hard for his father to arrange everything without him. Somehow, with the help of his neighbors he managed everything.

When any marriage happens in the villages then brothers and the relatives always have high expectations of being treated as kings. When the expectation is not met, most of the time people show their anger by not participating in the marriages. It happened with Reza. None of his brothers planned to participate in his son's marriage. He was little upset about this.

One of the villagers named Fazlu came to Reza and started talking to him.

Fazlu: I was thinking if any of the guests would ask you about why your brothers are not participating in your son's marriage, then what would you say?

Reza: I will tell him that they were not pleased with me.

Fazlu: This won't leave a good impression of you to the guests. They may think that you are not a good person.

Reza: Hmm. Then tell me what I should do.

Fazlu: You should go to your brothers, talk to them, and tell them to come on this happy occasion.

Reza: You are right. However, I don't think they will agree to it.

Fazlu: Somehow, you should make them agree.

Reza: I will try but I don't think they will.

Fazlu: When will you try?

Reza: I will go some day.

Fazlu: Why not now?

Reza: Will he be at home now?

Fazlu: He is at home.

Reza: Are you sure?

Fazlu: Yes, I've seen him this morning.

Reza: Ok, then let's go.

Both stood up and got ready to go to him. Rani was listening to their conversation behind the wall. She appeared to them covering her face. "Are you going empty handed? You should go with the invitation card and some laddu." Rani advised.

"You are right," Reza said, went inside and came out in few minutes with a small bag handy. They both went for Mujeeb's home.

Mujeeb was busy in worship in his room. One of his staff came, opened the door, and told them to sit on a chair.

"Who is this?" Fazlu asked pointing to the staff.

"He is a peon in the school but he lives in Mujeeb's house to serve him. In exchange for that, Mujeeb gives him food and he gave him a room in which to live." Reza informed him.

"How are you Fazlu?" Mujeeb asked.

"I am fine brother," Fazlu replied. "And how are you? Do you know that your nephew is getting married?" Fazlu added.

"Yes, I heard about it from the villagers but nobody has invited me yet." Mujeeb sarcastically replied.

"I came here to invite you," said Reza and took out the invitation card and laddu for him but Mujeeb stopped him with his hand.

"I was not asked at the time of the marriage proposal. Not even at the time of date setting. Now you come to invite me when the date of marriage is set and everything is finalized. Now how can you expect that I will accept your invitation?" Mujeeb was a bit angry in his tone so they both came back after a while.

The other teachers in the school were also told to not to participate in Reza's son's marriage.

Rani was lying on the bed. She was busy thinking about the different stages of her life. She was busy thinking of those days when she was not able to eat food of even her choice and many other problems, which she had to face. She faced all that only with the hope that the good days would come one day. She had a strong hope that when her son would be educated and he would become a valuable person in the society then she would live a good life. Moreover, whatever problem she faced her son would not encounter them. Now time was flying and the happy occasion of her son's marriage came. Very soon her son Anas would get married. Her son had earned a master's degree now. Those days were near when all of her dream would come true. Whenever she thought about her marriage, she could not stop her tears. This time also her face was wet with tears. She waited for a long time for happy days to come. She was getting older and because of her cough she felt accomplishing the daily routine work tough. However, she was happy that her son was getting married and soon another woman would come home and she would co-operate with her. Now she would get enough time to rest. She was busy thinking all that.

"Why are you lying on the bed? There are many things to do at home. Are you alright?" Reza opened the door and interrupted her. He knew that Rani couldn't sleep when she got emotional.

"O sorry, I am alright. What happened? What did he say?" Rani asked hiding her tears.

"He won't participate."

"I knew that he would say so." Rani replied and began coughing. Reza brought a glass of water and handed it over to her. She drank a little bit and Reza helped her to sleep on the cot.

"I don't know how long this bloody cough will hang on with me. It seems like it will go with my life," Rani told him with pain.

"Don't say this." Reza comforted her. "You need to live longer to see your son's marriage, his success and the days are yet to come when you will play with your grandkids." Reza added.

"I don't know. I really want to play with my grandkids. That will be amazing. I would like to share with you one very interesting thing." said Rani.

"What's that?" Reza asked with curiosity.

"I still have Anas's pants and a shirt which he wore when he was one year old. I kept them."

"Wow! Are you kidding?" Reza could not believe it. "How's that possible?" He was surprised.

"I will show you right now," said Rani and went to the box opened it and took out a piece of child's clothing. It was pink in color. Reza recognized it. "This is the one which I bought for Anas on his first birthday." He kept looking at the clothes with excitement. Rani was standing beside him and looking at Reza with pride as she accomplished something impossible.

"I will give it to the first child of Anas," said Rani with joy and put the clothes again in the same box.

The marriage took place. None of the teaching or non-teaching staff from Reza's school participated in the party. Many friends of Anas came but none of his friends from University came. There were many common friends of Hena and Anas who were expected to come but they did not show up. Later on Anas came to know that the friends who he had trusted were actually jealous of him because of his good result and because of his successful love marriage with Hena. They were in fact not friends they were only pretending to be friends.

After finishing *nikah*, the bride and groom came back home. This was Anas's home. Rani was standing at the door. She began crying with happiness. He sister was there to share the happiness with her on this auspicious occasion. The Hindu friends and neighbors of Rani were there to welcome the daughter-in-law home. The Hindu women had a big plate in their hands with a flame on it and many other ritual things including sandal wood powder. They took a pinch of the powder and put it on the daughter-in-law's forehead and then they welcomed her home. She came in then was introduced to the mother and father of Rani and other relatives.

When she came in, Rani was jumping with joy. She called Anas and gave him gold bangles, the most expensive thing she had, and told him to give it to Hena. Anas did so. When Rani went in Anas's room she saw Hena first. She was more beautiful than her expectation. As per the tradition, because she met the daughter-in-law for the first time she had to give some gift so she took out her gold ring and gave it to her.

After the marriage, Anas and his wife both went to Delhi. In the village after finishing the marriage party, all the relatives and friends left. Routine life began. Reza started going to his school. A few of the teachers came to meet him when he was alone and said that they could not participate because it was an order from his boss Mujeeb.

Rani kept busy cleaning their home and cooking food. A few neighbors came to her too to tell her that she is alone and will be alone because her only son had taken his wife with him and did not think about her life. She heard them and convinced them somehow that it was a necessity for him to take his wife with him.

Chapter Twenty

Now Anas was busy searching for a job. He had done all his study in the Urdu language so he could not find any job. There was a time in India when all the jobs were based on the local languages. However, this was time when one could not get a single job without learning English. Therefore, he struggled a lot and finally found a job in a call center where he had to go to the office on night shifts. He was happy because he had a job. His parents used to come to meet Anas and his wife every year. Life was going fine. Sometimes there was a cultural clash between Hena and Reza because Reza always thought of saving money while Hena was not ready to compromise with her or her family's daily needs. However, Rani was very smart in handling the situation so whenever Reza got angry she made him understand that he grew up in very poor family but the new generation was not like that. Why should they let their children be in trouble? This is their life so let them live happily. Eventually Reza also agreed with her.

In the call center, Anas found his life very difficult. His job was in Gurgaon where most of the call centers were based. He had to travel all the way from south Delhi to Gurgaon. The company had provided him a cab facility so he had to travel by cab. The travel time was equal to his job hours so he could not get time for anything except sleeping. In India, working in odd shifts was yet to be accepted. For the people from villages like Rani it was not less than a fight with poverty.

"This is not the result for which I spent my whole life in waiting. I did not want my son to work like this after getting higher education," said Rani when Anas entered his room. He did not expect that his mother would not be sleeping at the wee hour. It was 3:30 am. Anas did not have a good day today. He had argued with his boss about his work performance.

"Are you aware Ammi?" replied Anas.

"What kind of job are you doing? This was not the job, I dreamed about for you. Have you seen your face in the mirror? Your eyes are so red. I wasted all my struggles of life. I could not do anything better for you my son. This is all, my mistake," said Rani.

"Ammi, our good days will come one day but for the time being I have to do this work so I can survive in this cruel world," replied Anas.

"Hmm, Good days will come. Waiting for good days your father and I had struggles so much that you cannot even imagine. You passed your master degree. What happened about the professor kind of job?" asked Rani.

"There are thousands of people who have much higher qualifications than me. They will be given a chance first and when I finish my PhD, I will also be able to apply for any University but for now, I have to wait. Not much time six more months . . ." Before Anas completed his sentence Rani spoke up. "Then you will become a professor, right?" Rani completed his sentence.

"No Ammi, after that I will be able to apply for that kind of job. Many people have completed their PhDs and they will be given a chance first. But I am hopeful that one day I will become a professor and I will fulfill your dream." Anas assured his mom.

"I will die till then." Rani spoke with hopelessness and pulled up her blanket pretending that she was sleeping.

"You are going to live long. You won't die until you see me succeed." Anas said and went into his room where his wife was waiting for him. He ate his dinner and went to bed.

Rani could not sleep. She looked at Reza. She wanted to talk to him but he was in a deep sleep. They came to Delhi from their village to meet with Anas and his family. After celebrating Eid she had a plan to go back to the village with Reza. They were here for more than ten days. Reza's job did not allow him to be away for more than that.

Almost after one hour, Reza woke up for his routine prayer. He heard Rani crying. He came near to her and asked her what happened.

"Tomorrow we will go back to our village and after that again the same loneliness. Here when Anas comes I wake up, ask a few questions and talk to him. I won't be able to do so from now onward," she said crying.

"That's true but we can't take Anas with us he. He is not a small child he has his family. Try to understand." Reza tried to comfort her.

"For a mother, child is always a child no matter how big he grows." she replied.

Anas heard his mother's cry so he came out of his room too.

"What happened to her?" he asked Reza.

"Nothing, she is not feeling well." replied Reza. Rani began coughing again. It was very bad this time.

"I think you should get a proper diagnosis for her from a good doctor," said Anas.

"I've been to a doctor but he was not a good doctor. It seems like he misdiagnosed her and treated her with wrong medicines for more than six months. After his treatment, her condition turned worse." Reza informed him.

Anas had no money with him so he did not offer her treatment in Delhi. He suggested his father go back to the same doctor and tell him that there was no improvement. They needed to do the tests again to find what was going on exactly. I will try to send some money to you too for this task," suggested Anas.

"It's a good idea," said Reza.

The next morning was Tuesday, a week off for Anas. This was the day for the departure of Reza and Rani to the village as well. Hena was not very happy to see Anas caring so much about his parents. She wanted him to prefer focusing on family matters.

Anas was a little bit sad because his parents were leaving. As per the corporate rule, he was unable to avail leave for more than a week's time so he could not visit his hometown in the near future. It usually took twenty hours for him to go to his hometown; almost two days to go and two days to come by train. Moreover, his wife would not be able to live in New Delhi, the unfamiliar city. He knew that he would not be able to see his parents before the next Eid and they did too.

Anas waved his hands to his parents and returned to his home. While coming back he thought that again from tomorrow onwards he would be busy with the same schedule, same daily boring routine and the same lecture of the unfriendly boss about productivity. He wanted to get out of the boring life but there was no other option he had for now.

Chapter Twenty-One

Anas was coming from the old Delhi railway station. He was very sad because his parents left. He had no idea when he would see them again. He questioned why God had done this injustice to his family. He made his mother lame, his father a poor man and him a corporate employee, where life is hell. When he was passing through the post office he remembered that Shariq's elder brother used to live there. "I should go visit his brother and ask about how Shariq's life is going nowadays," he thought and moved in the busy street where an old big broken wooden gate welcomed him. He went inside the gate where there were two rooms but both were locked. He tried to find out with the neighbors nearby but nobody gave any information.

He became a little sad then he thought about Shariq's mother. Wow! What a feudal kind of lady she was! Don't know where she is nowadays.

"God has done one good thing to this world and that is he made mother. Mother is such an amazing relationship, and perhaps the only relationship that is pure. How do the people live who do not have mother?" He kept thinking random things. He saw a beggar, an old lady. She had on a worn dirty white sari and from the backside; she looked exactly like Shariq's mother.

Anas thought to give the lady a few coins. He went nearer to her and gave her the coins. She hid her face with her sari. She was very old. She took the coin and smiled. "May God provide you safety and fill your life with joy my son." Anas found this voice known; he recognized the voice and wanted to see the lady's face. However, the lady was hiding her face intentionally from him. When he noticed that she was trying to hide her face, his curiosity increased and he tried harder to see her but she did not let him. He moved from there and he hid himself to see her face. She looked exactly like Shariq's mother.

"How can she be here? It is not possible for her to sit at this dirty place in that dirty sari and broken slippers. She used to be a fashionable lady, very clean and serious. This lady must be her look-alike." He thought but he came back before her again and this time he recognized her. She was Shariq's mother. What is she doing here? Why is she in this position? Why is she in Delhi and why is she begging? All these questions rushed in his mind. He wanted answers to his questions. He came nearer to her. She again tried to hide herself from him.

"Why are you trying to hide? I already recognized you. Why are you begging and where is Shariq?" Anas asked all these questions in one breathe.

"How easy it is for you to ask all these questions and how difficult it is for me to answer. God! Why did you send this man to see me in this situation? I beg you not to laugh at me. Please don't." Her wrinkled face was wet with tears.

Anas took her face in his hands and told her, "I am not here to hurt you. I want to hear what happened to you. What forced you to be here? Where is Shariq?"

"Shariq is in jail. One day, the police came to my house. That was Friday, a black Friday. A police officer entered my home. I was at the door. There were many. They came in a jeep. Two of them came and grabbed Shariq. He was preparing for his exam. When I asked them not to do so, one of them kicked me and I fell down. When Shariq saw me falling down, he jumped and tried to free himself. Suddenly, they started beating him and took him in the jeep. It's been three years now. He is in jail."

"But why did the police do so?"

"The police think that he is a terrorist."

"But how can the police do so? There is a law and the police cannot arrest anyone like this."

"Yeah it used to happen; now anything is possible. To prove him innocent, I had to hire a lawyer. There was no source of income. The legal fight was so expensive that I had to sell my house in Muzaffarpur. I could not afford the travelling cost so I moved to Delhi. Here, Shariq's brother was killed by robbers and I was left alone to bear all this. Moreover, everywhere people see me and say look she is the mother of a terrorist. The newspapers and television talk about my son and I can't tell you how painful is my life. Yesterday, the court proved him innocent. However, I lost everything in the battle. Tomorrow, Shariq will get out of jail. All day, I sit here and ask people to help me. In the evening, I go home and sleep. From tomorrow onward, my life will get back on track. I am fortunate that it took only three years. There are people whose mothers wait for many years. Some of them die in this long wait. Tell me about your life. Why did you not come to meet us after that and how is Hena?"

"I did not know anything about all of this. Hena also lives here in Delhi. I will come tomorrow and help you to go to jail to receive Shariq."

The next morning there was a big headline in the newspaper that Shariq was killed in a police encounter. Anas ran to Old Delhi but he could not find the elderly lady. The neighbors told him that she did not come last night.

What a romantic person Shariq was and how sad was his life's story. No one would imagine that he would die this way. It was a fake encounter. The commission set up by the central government to inquire about it. What was the inquiry worth? It no longer made any difference whether the encounter was fake or real.

This was the reality of life. Anas was very upset. He went to his office and was working on the computer, but his mind was not there. His team leader called him in a meeting and gave him a final ultimatum that he needed to perform in the next few weeks otherwise the company would ask Anas to leave.

"Why will the company ask me leave where they can terminate? If the company terminates an employee then the company needs to pay all grievances like provident funds and two month's salary according to law. Therefore, they always ask you to leave and if you don't they take your ID card and they won't let you in for fifteen days and after that they declare you absconded."

It is not just. Many things in this world are not just. The situation with Shariq's mother was not just. The situation with Shariq, three years in jail and then death in a fake encounter was not just either. The whole world is running around injustice. What is the root of all these. There is much hatred, jealousy and cruelty, and the innocent people pay the price.

When Anas saw the news headline, his eyes became red and wet. He could not stop the tears. Hena saw him sad so she came by. She wanted to know why Anas was emotional. She saw the headline too. She started talking about how romantic and worry-free Shariq had been. She recalled the student life, the days in the college, when they met for the first time, and the beautiful poetry he used to sing in a sweet voice. His voice was now stopped. Why is this world against love and these kinds of lovely people? What was Shariq's fault? What is the fault of so many people in the world like Shariq who did not do anything wrong but are punished? Is God unjust? No, God can't be unjust.

Thank God that our life is peaceful. I am concerned about my children's future. Anas thought about Shariq's mother. Where could she be? How hopeful she was about her son, and what does she have? Thinking about Shariq's mother reminded Anas about his mother. He called his mother and talked to her. Anas's mother was very happy to talk to him. Reza was a little bit angry at Anas but Rani was not at all. Rani told him to call again and to call from time to time. She told that it makes her happy when she talks to him.

The day was not a good day for Anas and his wife. They both became sad and nostalgic after hearing the bad news about Shariq.

Rani had to go to see the doctor for a routine check-up. She did not feel any problem except coughing badly. She went to see her mother and father before going to Patna to see the doctor. Anas was aware that his mother was going to see the doctor as she had told him on the latest telephone conversation.

Chapter Twenty-Two

Rani and Reza were in the hospital. One of the doctors told them to go for certain tests. They were running out of money but their courage wasn't. After the tests were done, they were waiting for the reports. While the reports were being prepared they were asked to sit and wait in the waiting room.

"Why do people raise their sons and daughters? I think they do so, because they know when they become older their children will take care of them. But our only child doesn't have time to take care of us." Reza kept talking and Rani fell asleep. When Reza realized that she was not listening to him talk then he shook her. She woke up.

"Why do you think so? You will see. One day he will become a professor and he will have more money and a lot of time to take care of us. Our waiting will not go in vain."

"I don't think so. What I think is that he does not care about us. He has his wife and children to take care.

In his life, he has everything. Why would he need his old parents? We are worthless to him, only a burden." Reza tried to convince her but she did not reply. She only moved her neck to say no and tried to utter some words but she could not. In the mean time, a doctor called her name to give the report. Reza stood up and went to the doctor's room.

"Is everything ok, doctor?"

"No, not at all, she actually has the tuberculosis again."

"What? Can tuberculosis repeat?"

"Yes, it may. And when it repeats, then the chances of survival are minimized."

"What does it mean?"

"You did not make it in time sir."

"Hmm, what can be done now?"

"Nothing . . . only God knows how long she will live."

Reza sat down on the floor, took off his specs and wiped his eyes. He took out his mobile phone from his pocket and dialed the phone number of his son Anas, but he did not make the call. He disconnected and put the phone back in his pocket. When he came to Rani, she asked, "What happened?" Reza tried to hide but failed.

~~~

Anas was in the office. The team leader was not happy with his performance again. Today he missed his life in the village a lot. The team leader scolded him badly and told him not to come to the office if his performance continued this way. At the same time, he felt a little bit happy, too, because the next day began a week off, and his previous boss had invited him for dinner. During the break, he thought to call his mother to find how was she doing. When he called, he heard his father crying on the other side.

"Your mother is in the hospital in Patna. The doctor has said that the chance of her survival is nominal so come home as soon as possible." Anas was very upset. His anxiety level increased. As soon as he reached his boss's house, he began making calls to book a ticket, but it was not easy to get a ticket on the Indian railway. Finally, one of his friends who worked for the railway was able to get him a ticket for a special summer train leaving the next day.

Early in the morning the phone rang. Hena picked up the phone. Anas almost ran from his bed and grabbed the phone. He wanted to talk to his mother. Reza, his father, handed the phone over to Rani. She wanted to say many things but she only said, "I will tell you, I will talk to you later." Reza took the phone and informed Anas that she was not in a good position so she had to go for treatment.

After one hour, Anas got a call again. Reza told him that he should not come to Patna. They were going home. Anas understood and began crying bitterly. Hena snatched the phone from him and confirmed the death of Rani.

The train left at nine o'clock in the morning, and they reached home the next day at night about 1:00 am.

~∞∞∞~

Anas felt lonely in this world without his mother.

Within one year of her death, Reza married a second time. His new wife was a widow. He did not inform his son Anas about his marriage. He even stopped picking up his phone calls.

After five years, Anas completed his education. The wait for the good days to come continued. He had not been employed anywhere yet. As per the Islamic law, because his mother died while his father was alive, Anas forfeited his rights to receive his part of the property from his maternal grandfather.

Rani left a lonely son in the world. It did not matter that he had a wife and children; he did not have a mother. He struggled for his livelihood and he had no father even though his father was alive. He was very sad. He looked at a signboard. "Two drops to prevent Polio." He smiled and walked away to an unknown destination.

~∞∞∞~

You may send your feedback to the author regarding the story on <u>anwar.ra.jmi@gmail.com</u>.

~∞∞∞~